DEATH TO THE UNDEAD

By
Pembroke Sinclair

United States of America

Copyright 2012 PEMBROKE SINCLAIR
All Rights Reserved.

Cover Artist: Jerrod Brown
Byline and Title Design: Christy Caughie

No part of this book may be reproduced, stored in a retrieval system, or transmitted in any format or by any means without express written consent from the publisher. This book in electronic format may not be re-sold or re-distributed in any manner without express written permission from the publisher.

First Publication.
ISBN 978-1-937809-22-5

Published in the United States of America
Published by
eTreasures Publishing, LLC
4442 Lafayette St., Marianna, FL 32446
http://www.etreasurespublishing.com

This book is entirely fiction and bears no resemblance to anyone alive or dead, in content or cover art. Any instances are purely coincidental. This book is based solely on the Author's vivid imagination.

This ebook is licensed for your personal enjoyment only. This ebook may not be re-sold or given away to other people. If you would like to share this book with another person, please purchase an additional copy for each recipient. If you're reading this book and did not purchase it, or it was not purchased for your use only, then please return to **eTreasurespublishing.com** and purchase your own copy. Thank you for respecting the hard work of this author.

Acknowledgments

Once again, I would like to thank Jerrod Brown, horror artist, for the fabulous cover.

Dax, your support and insight are always invaluable.

Thanks also to everyone at eTreasures who continue to believe in me and my books.

Death To The Undead

CHAPTER 1

"Rome wasn't built in a day." God, I can't tell you how many times I've heard that cliché. Dad was particularly fond of it when I had issues with homework or a dilemma in my personal life. I knew what his point was. He was telling me to be patient, to let things progress the way they were supposed to. But, I wasn't good at that. I never had a lot of patience. I imagined my Dad reiterating the cliché after the North Platte takeover, wondering what he would think of what I'd done. What we'd done. We liberated Nebraska, but we still had a long road ahead of us. I knew Rome wasn't built in a day, but I was pretty sure the zombies could destroy it in one.

I stood in the guard tower, overlooking the field. My body pressed against the railing. Corpses still littered the ground, but there weren't as many as when I first came to North Platte. The crews had done a great job of cleaning up, though there was little they could do about the atrocious smell.

The sun sank beneath the horizon, casting hues of orange, pink, and purple onto the silhouettes of the undead. A bullet was chambered into a gun behind me. Quinn had been sitting in a chair behind me in the tower the whole time.

"Quinn, what happened to your parents?" I turned so I faced him.

Quinn rested the butt of his gun on the deck and wrapped his arms around the barrel. He sighed. "My mom died about seven years ago from cancer. I don't know what happened to my dad."

I furrowed my brow. "What do you mean?"

"Well, when we heard about the first zombie attacks, Dad wanted to help. Most of the neighbors lived within a few miles, so it didn't take too long for him to move them onto the ranch. One morning, him and a few of the others decided to venture a little further, see who else might need some help, and he never came back."

My stomach felt queasy. I averted my gaze to the floor, then glanced back at Quinn. "Did you go look for him?"

Quinn shook his head. "He told me not to. He said no matter what happens, I was to stay at the ranch and take care of the people."

"Yeah, but you must have been curious what happened to him."

Quinn nodded and stood from his chair. "Of course, but I did as I was told." He shouldered the rifle and lined up his sights. He fired.

I moved so I stood next to him. "Do you think he's out there somewhere?"

Quinn glanced at me. "Probably. But I doubt he's anything like I remember."

"Doesn't that make you sad?"

He returned his attention to the sight. "Every day. But there's nothing I can do to change it now." He fired another round.

I slumped against the rail. Tears welled up in my eyes, and I averted my gaze back to the field. I rubbed my sore shoulder. A breeze picked up, bringing a chill and the smoke from the funeral pyre. I wrinkled my nose.

"We need to do something about that."

Quinn straightened. "Like what?"

I shrugged the good shoulder. "I don't know. Maybe we could put a building around it. It might help contain some of the smoke and smell."

Quinn nodded. "You should suggest it at the next meeting."

I opened my mouth to speak, but the sound of footsteps on the stairs interrupted me. It was Pam. She still wore her old guard uniform, a relic from Liet's reign, but it was obvious whose side she was on. Thank goodness she was on our side. She trained me; I knew how tough and skilled she was. It would've been a battle to take her down.

"Krista," Pam said. "There's someone who needs to see you."

I pushed myself away from the rail. "Who?"

Pam motioned toward the courthouse. "I think it's best if you just head over there."

I looked at Quinn, who shrugged, then the three of us headed to the courthouse.

My stomach fluttered as I pushed opened the door. Visions of Mrs. Johnson's bodyguard flooded my mind, and I didn't think I could stand another visit like that. I held my breath as I opened the door. The person stood at the end of the room, her head down as she chewed on her thumb nail. Excitement rose in my chest and relief loosened my shoulders. A smile crossed my lips. I held out my good arm and hurried across the room. Normally, I wasn't one for hugs, but anyone besides guards from Florida in the office was a welcome relief.

"Tanya! What are you doing here?"

Tanya looked up. She balled her hand into a fist and swung it over her head. I flinched, and the blow hit me on the bicep. Tanya lunged forward, flailing her arms. I crouched and covered my head. I didn't know what else to do. I was so shocked, I froze. I couldn't react. Several more hits landed on my back and head before someone pulled Tanya away.

"How could you?" Tanya yelled. "HOW COULD YOU?" She kicked and caught me on the knee.

Pain radiated through my leg, and I rubbed at the minor injury. Anger replaced the shock. Who did she think she was coming into my courtroom and attacking me?

"What are you talking about?" I tried to keep my emotions in check, common sense told me I needed to know what was going on.

"Don't play dumb with me! You know what you did." She jerked her arms out of Quinn and Pam's grasp.

Death To The Undead

Really? Was she mad that we liberated Nebraska before we helped Florida? I didn't think it was a big deal, but I guess it upset her.

"I'm sorry, Tanya. We had to move quickly. We had to set the people of North Platte free."

She narrowed her eyes. "I'm not talking about the attack."

I stared at her for a moment. "Then what are you talking about?"

"You sent zombies down in the truck of supplies! You figured if you couldn't overthrow The Families, you'd overrun the state with the undead!" Tanya yelled, then attempted to attack again. Pam and Quinn restrained her and stared at me.

I picked myself off the floor, staring at Tanya wide eyed. Zombies in the truck? What? When? Why would I have done that? I hate those things! I would have to get pretty close to put those in the truck, and I wasn't willing to do that. But someone must have. Who would be stupid and conniving enough to do that?

"Tanya, honestly, I have no idea what you are talking about. Maybe you should fill us in on some details."

Tanya snarled. "The truck showed up a few weeks ago, with Mrs. Johnson's bodyguard behind the wheel. He said it had come from North Platte, and I assumed it had another shipment of guns. As usual, I was going to wait until night to collect the weapons. My father took the vehicle to the storage yard, like he always did. I was done working at the coffee shop, so I decided to see what you guys sent. I stood at the chain link fence, watching the guys work, when I heard my father scream from the trailer. The others ran to see what was going on, and a zombie lurched out of the vehicle. They ran."

Tanya continued her story, and I pictured the whole scenario in my mind. She was a bit lacking on details, so I filled in the blanks with my own imagination. It wasn't hard, especially when you've seen as many zombies as I have. There were three creatures, buried under crates. Two men, newly turned with just the slightest hint of yellowed skin. Their clothes were dirty but not yet torn. The third, a woman, she had been a zombie for a while. Her stringy blonde hair was knotted, caked in mud, and falling out of her head, only wisps remained on the bottom and right side. Her clothes had almost completely decayed, tatters of a floral print dress clung to her the bones exposed in her chest and legs. Her gray, wrinkled skin looked like leather. They hid in the shadows, hard to see, and for some reason, they didn't moan like the others when food was near. The workers didn't know they were there and had unloaded almost the entire truck. They were almost finished when the attack started. Tanya ran through the gate, making her way to the back of the truck, just in time to see her father beating one of the creatures with a tire iron. The third one was still pinned behind a crate. Her breath caught as she watched the creature's mouth snap for her dad. Her dad panted with exhaustion. He leaned against the side of the truck for support. Blood, brain matter, and bits of skull were everywhere, and the smell was overpowering. Tanya was about to climb in, find out if her dad was all right, but he told her to stop. He collapsed onto the floor, sliding down the wall. He cradled his hand. The zombie had bitten him.

Tanya set her jaw. "The other one that got out of the truck attacked several of the workers before it was put down. I don't know how many of them got bit, but within a few days, we had an epidemic on our hands. They got it under control, but thirty people got infected."

Pam and Quinn released her, and she pointed a finger in my direction.

"You just couldn't wait, could you? You just had to make all of us pay."

My throat felt tight and a knot developed in my stomach. I swallowed hard. "What happened to your dad?"

Tanya snarled. "Instead of waiting for the plague to take its toll, he took care of himself."

I lowered my gaze to the floor. My stomach lurched, bile rose into my throat. I took several deep breaths, but the feeling never abated.

"I'm sorry, Tanya." I looked into her face. "I really, truly am. But I did not put zombies in the back of the truck. Why would I harm the people I'm trying to help?"

Tanya shook her head and opened her mouth to speak.

"Think about it," Quinn interrupted her. "The Families were afraid of losing control. They knew about the rebellion here in North Platte, and they knew the people would soon hear about it. They had to do something to ensure the people wouldn't revolt, so they planted zombies."

Tanya stared at him for a moment, letting the information sink in. "Maybe," she spoke softly.

I stepped closer to her. "Tanya, please, you have to believe us, we would never do anything like that. Smuggle guns to kill the regime, yeah, but we wouldn't infect Florida with zombies."

Tanya took a deep breath. "Maybe."

"Didn't Bill and Kyle tell you what was going on?" Quinn asked.

Tanya faced him. "They did."

"What happened to them?"

She took a deep breath and averted her gaze to the floor. "After the attack and my dad's suicide, guards, um, did random house searches and they were arrested."

Pam's, Quinn's, and my eyes grew wide.

"What?" Quinn glanced from Tanya to me. "Arrested? Why?"

"They were outsiders." she responded. "I guess they felt they were a threat to The Families and Florida."

"Did they find out about the guns?" I stammered out the question.

Tanya looked at me. "No. Those are still safe."

"How did you get here?" Pam chimed in.

"After everything calmed down, I took the boat Bill and Kyle came in on and found their vehicle in Texas. I made my way up here to you."

"Do you know what happened to them?" Worry coated Quinn's eyes.

"I'm sure they're not dead. I'm sure The Families kept them for interrogation."

Quinn rubbed his hand over his mouth, staring at me. "What are we going to do? Everything is ruined. I told you we had to attack simultaneously."

Confusion and anger coursed through my body. "It's a moot point now. We'll figure it out. It'll be fine." What did he expect me to do? I couldn't change the past.

The room was silent for a long moment. The group glanced at each other out of the corners' of their eyes, then averted their gazes to the floor. My head spun. When we first took over North Platte and found out there had been a spy, I felt like I was losing control then, but after Tanya arrived, I knew I lost my grip. An all-out attack on Florida was out of the question. They would know what was coming. Plus, we were grossly outnumbered by Floridian soldiers. Despite the tragic nature of the event, a zombie attack wasn't a half bad idea. It would keep the soldiers busy long enough for our people to get in and take control. There would be some collateral damage, but in the long run, it would lead to the liberation of the people of Florida.

I shook the idea out of my head. How could I even think of that? There were innocent people down there. Children. It wouldn't work. Besides, three zombies had already done enough damage. I couldn't believe Tanya thought we sent the attack.

Quinn grabbed my arm and directed me away from Tanya and Pam.

"We've got to evacuate the city."

"Why?"

"Don't you see what's going on? Florida sent men up here to investigate what happened. They planted zombies in the back of the truck and blamed it on us. They are trying to rally the masses against us."

"Yeah? So what else is new?"

"The people they sent here were the dregs of society. They were causing problems in Florida. They are still causing problems. This is the perfect excuse to wipe us off the planet."

My stomach knotted. The color drained from my face. I didn't want to believe it, but I knew Quinn was right. They were probably on their way to level the city.

"There are two thousand and eleven people in North Platte." I couldn't raise my voice over a whisper. "Where are they going to go?"

Quinn pinched the bridge of his nose between his thumb and forefinger and shook his head. "I don't know. All I know is they can't stay here."

"What about Liet? What are we going to do with him?"

Quinn didn't have the opportunity to answer.

"Everything all right over there?" Pam asked.

We faced her.

"No. I don't think it is," Quinn responded.

"Well, maybe you'd like to fill the rest of us in."

Quinn glanced at me for a second, then back at Pam. "I think you need to call a town meeting."

"For what?"

"Just do it!" I didn't mean to yell at her, but I had no control over my emotions. The room spun and breathing was difficult, it just slipped out.

Pam hurried out of the room, and I sank to my knees. I lowered my head and closed my eyes. I felt light-headed and nauseous. I couldn't believe it was this hard. It wasn't supposed to be this hard. I felt Quinn's hand on my back.

"You all right?"

I looked up at him. "I'll be fine. Just give me a second."

Tanya moved so she stood in front of me. Her knees popped as she knelt down.

"What are we going to do now? Everything has been ruined." She lowered her gaze. "I ruined it. I can't believe I was so stupid to believe you would have sent zombies!"

I took a deep breath and stared at her face for several moments. Anger clenched my chest. I wanted to tell her it was her fault, that she should have known we would never do anything so devious, but it wouldn't get us anywhere. Her eyes were red rimmed and her shoulders slumped forward. She probably didn't stop traveling until she made it to the city. Rage kept her moving. Her desire to see me dead or maimed fueled her journey. After she found out the truth, rage was replaced with sheer exhaustion. Sadly, her journey wasn't even close to being over.

Besides, I wasn't mad at her, I was angry at the universe. I was upset that my luck had run out. The same rage that kept her moving was going to have to sustain me. We still had a job to do, we just had to rethink it.

"You didn't ruin it," I told her. "You were just reacting to a situation you thought we created. It's understandable."

She placed her hands on the floor and leaned forward. "I want to help you fix it. Please tell me what I can do."

"First of all, we've got to get the people to safety. Then, we're going to disappear."

"And go where?"

"The only place we have left. The West."

Death To The Undead

CHAPTER 2

I hated speaking in public. Especially when I thought the crowd would turn into a lynch mob and scream for my head. Quinn tried to make me feel better. He told me the people of North Platte knew what they were getting into when they rebelled, and in the back of my mind, I knew he was right. But he wasn't the one on the podium. He wasn't the one delivering the bad news. The one thing I hoped was that with my arm still in a sling, the workers would feel sorry for me.

The crowd gathered in the high school gym. I stood on a soap box in the middle of the basketball court, facing the bleachers with a bull horn in my hand. As I stared at the crowd, I tried to pinpoint the men and women I thought would rush me first. I cleared my throat and brought the bull horn to my mouth.

"First of all, I would like to thank you all for coming." My voice cracked through the mouthpiece. Thankfully, the horn covered the majority of my face. My cheeks and ears turned red. "As I'm sure some of you are aware, we had a visit from Florida within the past few weeks." I expected the crowd to burst into hushed whispers amongst themselves, but I was met with silence. I carried on. "We have reason to believe they are planning an attack. Perhaps planning on wiping us off the face of the earth." I paused and flinched, expecting angry roars from the crowd. Again, I was met with silence. "We think the safest course of action is to leave North Platte. We think we should head into the West." I lowered the bullhorn. It was out now. If they were going to get angry, I couldn't stop it.

Quinn sat in the front row, and I found his gaze. He nodded and gave me a thumbs up. I turned my attention back to the crowd, a knot developed in my stomach. I would have preferred them angry and yelling at me. At least then they would have reacted. All of them sitting there in silence made me nervous. Was I supposed to give them more information? Were they expecting something else from me?

"Is there anyway we can be sure they are coming here to destroy us?" A voice spoke from the crowd.

I looked up to see a woman, probably in her mid-twenties, with a blonde-haired, blue-eyed boy on her lap.

I shook my head. "No. Unfortunately, it's all speculation at this point."

"Then why should we leave on speculation?" It was an older man, close to 60, who wore a plaid shirt and sat with his arms crossed over his chest.

I shrugged. "That choice is up to you. I'm just telling you what we know. Or what we think we know. After the group from Florida left here, Tanya," she sat next to Quinn and I pointed her out, "came here to tell us about a zombie infestation." I told them the story about the zombies in the truck and how they attacked in the storage yard. After I finished, I was met with silence again, but the crowd looked at one another, searching each other's faces for an answer or more information.

Quinn stood from his seat and faced them. "What Krista is saying is that it's better to be safe than dead. We don't know for sure that they are coming to destroy us, but we have to plan for the worst-case scenario. Would any of you put it past The Families to see you dead?"

Members of the crowd shook their heads.

"They sent you here for a reason," Quinn continued. "And now you are a threat to their power and means of control. They have already tried to rein in the people of Florida, to keep them afraid, what do you think their next logical step is going to be?"

"Why the West?" the woman with the child asked. "Why not somewhere further east? Maybe up north?"

"You know," I said, "anywhere you choose to go outside of North Platte will be safer. But if Florida realizes you're gone and wants to hunt you down, they probably won't stop looking for you in the east or up north. I'm pretty sure they'll hesitate coming after you in the West."

"Where are we going to go in the West?" A teenager with stringy brown hair asked. "There are thousands of us."

"And there are completely abandoned cities," Quinn interjected.

"But they've been overrun with zombies." The teenager's voice squeaked. "How are we going to defend against that?"

His question got the crowd talking. They turned to each other, looking for answers, and they shot a multitude of questions down at Quinn and I, most of them I couldn't understand. Quinn grabbed the bullhorn from me.

"People!" His loud voice quieted the crowd. "We understand your concerns, and we're not sending you out there unarmed or unprepared. You've dealt with the zombie menace day in and day out, it's not any different over there."

"But there are more of them and we don't have a wall to help protect us." I scanned the crowd, but couldn't tell who the speaker was.

"Yeah, there are more of them, but they aren't unstoppable. They are slow, they are dumb. If you are smart, you will survive out there. You will have protection and shelter. It's not like we're leaving here without a plan."

"Then what is the plan?" the man in the plaid shirt asked.

Quinn handed the bullhorn back to me.

"We are going to gather every supply we can find. Every gun, every can of food, every extra scrap of clothing, and anything else you want to take, and we're loading it into the trucks. Once that is done, we'll head into Wyoming. There are small towns, tiny places, that the zombies haven't touched, surrounded by mountains that you will call a safe haven. The natural landscape will aid in your protection, and you can do anything else to make sure you feel safe."

"How long do we have?"

"Twenty-four hours. Anymore, and we risk Florida invading."

The crowd rose from their seats, filing out of the gym and talking to themselves. No one spoke to Quinn or I, but they nodded in our direction as they passed. I didn't draw an easy breath until the gym was almost empty.

Pam and Tanya stood from the bleachers and joined Quinn and I in the middle of the floor.

"That went pretty well," Pam stated.

I nodded. "Thank goodness."

She smiled. "Oh, we would have protected you for as long as possible if they had come after you."

Quinn smirked. "No one was coming after you. They knew what they were getting into when the picked up the guns and rebelled against Liet. C'mon. Let's get your stuff packed." He wrapped his arm around my shoulders and we headed toward the door.

As we stepped into the hallway, we were met by a group of 15 people standing in a circle, the mother and child and man with the flannel shirt in the center. They turned toward us. Great, just great. They waited for us in the hall. They didn't want to make a scene in the gym, so now they're going to exact their revenge. I hoped the worry and fear didn't show on my face.

"If we may have a moment," the mother said.

Quinn and I glanced at each other before focusing our attention back on them.

"Sure," he said. He didn't sound worried at all.

"I'm Lydia." The woman placed her hand on her chest. "And this is Chester. He and I, along with everyone else, just had a few more questions for you."

Quinn removed his arm from my shoulders and pushed his hands into his pockets. "I hope we can answer them for you."

"First of all, do you have an idea of where you want to take us?"

"It's a little town called Dashton. It's in Wyoming, but you won't find it on any map. It's tucked between some canyons. It was founded by bandits, and they wanted to remain hidden, so the town has, too."

More than likely, the people who founded the town were the same ones who created Quinn's ranch. I was sure they needed two different places, just in case one was compromised, but I imagined there were probably more. Of course, I didn't say anything out loud. I knew Quinn wanted to keep his place a secret. Even if these people were on our side, the fewer people who knew, the fewer could give directions if anything ever happened. Plus, I liked the idea of being able to vanish without anyone being able to find me. It would be like going on vacation if things got too out of hand.

"You're still planning on invading Florida, right?" Lydia wondered. "I mean, this isn't a turn tail and run and hope for the best. Some of our families are still down there."

My chest felt lighter and my knees went a little weak with relief as it flooded my body. I couldn't help but smile. "Of course we're still going after Florida. We just have to regroup and re-organize the plan."

Lydia took a deep breath, relief flooded over her face. "Thank goodness."

"We want to be part of the planning and the invasion," Chester stated. His tone implied it wasn't up for discussion and we couldn't deny him.

"We can use all the help we can get," I told him.

"Are there others who feel the same?" Quinn's eyebrows were pushed together, his expression serious. "Or is it just the fifteen of you?"

"Oh, it's pretty much everyone in town, with the exception of the kids." Chester was overly serious. "We also want to know what you're planning on doing with Liet and the others."

Quinn looked at me as he pulled his hand out his pocket and rubbed the back of his neck. He focused back on the group.

"We haven't decided on that. Do you guys have any suggestions?"

A smile curled onto Chester's face, deepening the wrinkles on his forehead. "Oh, yeah. We've got an idea, but I'm not so sure you're going to like it."

"Well, anything shy of killing him, we're willing to entertain."

"We wouldn't kill him exactly," Lydia looked at the others before focusing her gaze back on us. "We would just drop him somewhere in the West without any weapons and hope the zombies take care of him."

Surprisingly, I wasn't as shocked by her suggestion as I should have been. After all the pain, suffering, and heartache Liet caused, a little payback was in order. God knows how many men and women he sent to their deaths. Trust me, I entertained the idea many a times after we took over North Platte, I just didn't voice it out loud. I knew what Quinn would say, but there was also another issue with the plan: what if Liet survived? It was possible; people had been doing it in the West since the outbreak. Granted, his chances would be less without any weapons, but it wasn't impossible. Then what would he do? I'm pretty sure he would relentlessly hunt all of us down and kill us, maybe even torture us to death. It wasn't a risk I wanted to take. I didn't want to spend the rest of my life looking over my shoulder.

Besides, we weren't like him, so we didn't need to enact a punishment like he would. We were the future of the nation, and we needed to show a little compassion. The possibility existed that no one would know what we'd done, but we'd know. Could we in good conscience continue on knowing what we did to another human being? I couldn't speak for the group in front of me, but I was sure it would haunt me forever.

Quinn placed his hands back in his pockets. "Well, it's an idea to consider, though I can't guarantee one we'll employ."

Lydia shrugged. "We understand. We just wanted to put it out there."

Quinn nodded and smiled. "We appreciate it. We have a lot of work to do to leave the city, I suggest you get home and get your affairs in order. There will be plenty of time to talk about Florida and Liet later."

The group agreed and thanked us for our time before heading home.

"I guess I'll get my things together, too," Pam stated. With a salute, she headed to the women's house.

Tanya, Quinn, and I walked back to Liet's old apartment. Tanya plopped down on the couch.

"My stuff is already packed," she mumbled under her breath before focusing her attention on digging out dirt from under her nails.

"I'll help you with your stuff," Quinn said, and we headed to my room.

I stood in the doorway, staring at my belongings. At one point, I would have fought tooth and nail for them. It was my place of normal, the one area I could go to and feel safe, the one place that was all my own. As I contemplated what I should take, what was important, none of it seemed to matter. I felt like a stranger. Liet told me at one point that none of the stuff was really mine, it was his, he was just nice enough to let me have it. I argued with him about it, but as I looked around, he was right. None of the stuff had any meaning to me. It all reminded me of him and how much I hated being under his control. I looked at the stacks of CDs. Which ones would I want to listen to? Would I even have time to listen to them? Were there any in there Quinn could enjoy with me? I glanced at the closet. What kind of clothes would I need? How soon would winter be moving in? How cold would it get? How hot? Was there something in there Quinn thought I looked good in?

Quinn stood in the middle of the floor, his hands on his hips as he scanned the room. He found a bag and grabbed it.

"What do you want me to put in here?"

I shook my head. "Nothing."

"C'mon, now. You have to take something. Some clothes, a coat."

"Then you decide." I walked to the bed and sat down.

With a sigh, Quinn sat next to me. He placed a hand on my knee.

"Leaving can be difficult. Maybe a little scary. And it's hard to know what you'll need out there. But whatever you leave behind, we can replace."

"It's not the leaving that's hard," I spoke softly, my gaze focused on my lap. "I actually can't wait to get the hell out of here." I looked at his face. "It's figuring out what's important. I mean, do I need my CDs? In the scheme of things, when will I ever listen to them again? What kind of clothes do I need? Besides, they all remind me of Liet. Do I need to take that memory with me?"

Quinn placed a hand on my cheek before leaning forward and kissing me. When he pulled away, he rested his forehead against mine.

"No, you don't. We can make some memories of our own, and we don't need these things to do it. If you want to leave it all here, fine with me. We can find other stuff."

"And what are we going to do with Liet? Killing him would be the best option, then we wouldn't have to worry about him ever again, but I know we can't. The zombies have caused enough death, we don't need to add to the toll. And he could come in handy later."

Quinn sighed. "I don't know, Krista. I just don't know. Right now, we'll take him to Dashton. After Florida is taken care of, then we'll decide what to do with him."

"Okay. Sounds like a plan."

We stared at each other for a while longer. I didn't want the moment to end, but we had a lot of work ahead of us. Plus, my shoulder ached and I needed some pain pills. After I took those, I would be ready for bed. Quinn sensed my discomfort, and he pulled away.

"I should go and see if anyone else needs help." He hesitated, perched on the edge of the bed, but eventually he stood.

"Let me walk you to the door."

He stood at the open apartment door and leaned against the jamb. He took my good hand in his.

"Even though everything seems uncertain right now, just know that I'm going to be right here with you. You don't have to go through this alone."

His words, even though kind of corny, meant a lot. From the moment I lost my parents until I came to North Platte, I did feel like I was alone, like no one knew what I was going through. It was silly, I know, because we were all in the same situation. Every one of us was threatened or affected in some way by the zombie horde. But we all experienced it differently, and it was nice to know I had my very own support group. I placed my hand on his face.

"And I'm here for you."

He leaned forward and kissed me before heading out.

I closed the door and turned toward Tanya. She snored on the couch. I grabbed a blanket and covered her up. I stared at her for a moment, feeling sorry for her. She wanted to be apart of the revolution, but I highly doubted this was what she had in mind. I'm sure she wanted her dad alive, to be proud of her, to tell her what a good job she'd done. I knew how hard it was to lose a parent, especially because of some stupid decision or act. It was going to take her a long time to get over, if she ever got over it. I hoped she was like me, though, and I hoped she took all of her anger and resentment and sadness and focused it on one task. Preferably taking down Florida or maybe destroying the zombies in the West. Either way, she needed something to occupy her mind. It was the one thing that would keep her going.

Death To The Undead

It was the only thing that kept me going.

CHAPTER 3

It was easy getting the workers and the former guards organized to leave North Platte. They didn't have much, so it didn't take them long to pack. Once everything was ready, Quinn gave them instructions of where to go. He wanted the town empty for our final task. Even though he didn't think anything was going to happen, he didn't want to take the chance. There were still a lot of bad feelings toward Liet and the others who refused to convert.

I stood outside the door to the holding cells, my shoulder ached more than normal as I thought about facing my cousin. Quinn, Pam, and Tanya stood behind me.

"You sure you want to go in there alone?" Pam asked.

I nodded without looking at her. "Yeah. We need to subdue him first. He might get the others riled up." I couldn't tear my gaze away from the closed door.

"If anyone is going to rile him up, it's going to be you. You've always been the focus of his anger." Quinn's voice made it possible to break my stare. I looked at him.

"Well, I guarantee if you go in there, it will definitely upset him. Same with Pam. I'm pretty sure he won't hesitate trying to kill you. With any luck, he'll show some restraint with me. He doesn't know Tanya, and she's unaware of what he's capable of, so I don't want to send her in there." I took a deep breath. "This is really the only way."

Death To The Undead

Pam placed a hand on my good shoulder. "We're right here if you need us. Don't hesitate to call."

Quinn nodded. "We can be in there in a split second."

Tanya stared at me, her arms crossed over her chest, the look on her face told me she was undecided about coming to my rescue. I didn't blame her. We told her some stories about Liet, I'm sure she was scared to death. I smiled at the others.

"I won't hesitate if something goes wrong."

Taking another deep breath, I turned and grabbed the handle of the door. I pulled it open and stepped inside.

The cells lined the right side of the room. They were a lot like the cells we stayed in in Casper. The doors were constructed of metal bars, while the other three walls were concrete blocks. I looked down the rows of black bars. The only sound was my own breathing. Hands poked into the halls, resting on the bars, and eyes watched me, waiting to see what I was going to do. In all, about fifteen guards didn't want to be integrated into society and still held loyalty to Liet. They weren't much of a threat to the city, but to the four of us, it could be detrimental. Our best bet was to take the leader out first, make sure he couldn't inspire them to riot, then the others should fall in line nicely. At least, that's what we hoped. That's what I hoped. But I knew Liet wasn't one to go quietly. We placed him in the last cell at the end of the hall. Even though he was able to talk to the others, we hoped the distance from them would deter him. So far, he seemed to keep to himself.

Pembroke Sinclair

I made my way down the hall, well aware of the loud squeaks my shoes made on the linoleum floor. My heart rate increased and thumped in my ears. I wondered if others could hear it, too. I kept my gaze forward, my head high, trying to portray a confidence I didn't feel. I watched them from the corner of my eye, thinking--hoping--they wouldn't try anything. In reality, if they wanted to grab me, nothing stopped them. The room was just big enough that if I pressed myself against the wall, they couldn't reach me. But I wasn't pressed against the wall. I walked down the center of the floor. All these people knew was power, and if I attempted to portray it, maybe they would believe it. After all, we already overthrew them. They were the ones behind bars. If I skimmed against the wall, they would sense my fear and pounce on it. I needed to remain in control, even if it was an illusion.

I stopped in front of his cell. Liet sat on the edge of his bed, wearing his green fatigue pants and a ribbed white tank top. I was aware of the pin-up girl tattoos on his forearms, but I had never seen the ones on his upper arms. His right arm was toward me, and his shoulder was covered with the branches of a leafless tree. I followed the lines of the branches with my eyes, around his shoulder blade, until they were covered by his shirt. I figured the rest of the tree covered his back. From one of the limbs on his arm hung a guy. His body was limp and his eyes bulged, but his mouth was curled into a sinister smile. I shuddered. Liet stared at me.

"Well, well. Krista."

I heard the hate in his tone as he spoke my name.

"Her royal highness has left her mighty throne to pay us prisoners a visit." He stood from the bed and faced me.

I could see his other arm. Again, his shoulder was covered with bare branches, but a woman hung from this limb. She was naked and had the same sinister grin as the man, but she was also flipping the bird. I wondered for a second what the rest of the tattoo looked like, then decided I didn't want to know. I assumed it had something to do with why he was in jail, and I didn't need to hear the story. The only reason I thought that was because of the research I did as a kid, when I read about serial killers and other criminals. Some of them liked to document their crimes in ink on their body, albeit cryptically. They knew what it meant, but no one else did. I speculated, of course, because I didn't know. However, I wouldn't put anything past Liet. He obviously kept it covered when he liked me so he didn't scare me or have to talk about the past, but those days were gone. I'm sure he thought he intimidated me, standing there with his shoulders back and fists balled at his sides, like he was ready to pounce at any moment.

I probably should have been afraid. Logically, it was the proper emotional response. Liet wasn't large, he was pretty thin, but he did have muscles. He was what I would call wiry. Instead, I struggled to swallow down the laugh that threatened to escape. I had faced him, gone toe to toe, and even though I was injured, I still won. He was the one behind bars, the king who lost his kingdom. His posturing and body threats were wasted on me. Still, I was sure if we had a rematch, he would probably kill me. That thought made my stomach flutter and the laugher vanish from my lips.

"How does your arm feel?" he smirked.

I glanced at my sling, then back into his face. "It's getting better. You'd be amazed how fresh air aids in the healing process."

The smile dropped from his lips. "What are you doing here?"

"We're moving every one to the West."

"And you've come to say goodbye?" he hissed.

"Oh, you'd like that, wouldn't you? To be left behind so your friends from Florida can save you before leveling the town." I stepped closer to the door. "But that's not going to happen. We're taking you with us."

The thought had crossed Quinn's and my mind to leave Liet and the others here to their fate. It would have made our lives so much easier. But, again, there was the chance he could survive. I always heard you should keep your friends close and your enemies closer. I never knew what that meant until having to deal with Liet.

Liet threw his head back, a loud, raucous, forced laugh escaped from his mouth. "And you thought I'd be a good boy and let you cuff me and take me wherever you please?"

I stared at him with pursed lips, my hand on my hip. The nervousness and fear I felt in my stomach quickly hardened into anger. Who did this guy think he was? He was in no position to make threats. He acted like a child, and I was ready to put him back into place. I stepped closer to the door and placed my good hand on a bar.

"I'm pretty sure I wasn't asking if you wanted to come to the West." My voice was low, threatening. I was a little surprised at how much anger actually drifted out.

Liet stepped forward and placed his hand above mine. "And I'm pretty sure I won't be going quietly." His tone matched mine.

I couldn't help but smile. I was hoping, wishing, waiting for him to say that. I slid my hand from the bar and took one step back.

"This doesn't have to be like this. It can be simple and easy."

He leaned forward, squeezing his face between the bars. "It's never simple, and I'm definitely not going to make it easy. You want me to leave this cell, you're gonna have to shoot me."

I shrugged and reached into my sling. Pulling out the boxy taser, I pointed it at him. He didn't even have a chance to blink before I shot the electrodes at him. They hit his chest, and his body went stiff as the electricity flowed through him. His knees buckled, and he fell to the ground, spit dripping from his mouth.

"You bit-"

I pressed the button again, and his body stiffened. He rolled to the side, his back toward me. I seized the moment and grabbed his right arm. I took the cuffs out of my sling and slapped one end around his wrist, the other hung free. He took deep, ragged breaths and looked over his shoulder at me, a smile snaked onto his lips.

"How are you gonna get my other arm?"

Without saying a word, I unlocked his door, slamming the metal into his back. He arched as the pain ricocheted through his spine and groaned. I hit him again, and he rolled on his stomach, out of the way. I hit him with another jolt of electricity. After 30 seconds, I stepped into his cell and grabbed his left wrist. With one hand, I had him cuffed and ready for transport. He huffed and wheezed on the floor. He tried to gnash his teeth at me, to roll over and get the upper hand, but his body wouldn't cooperate. I sat on the small of his back and patted him between his shoulder blades.

"You brought this all on yourself, just remember that. I was willing to take it easy on you."

I set the taser next to him, and heard the footsteps coming down the hall. I stepped out of the cell and faced Quinn and Pam.

"Anyone else want to take the hard way?" I taunted.

In reply, hands poked through the cell doors, their fingers intertwined and ready for cuffs.

The plan was to transport the prisoners in the back of a semi. It wasn't ideal, but we didn't have any other choice. There were only four of us, and 15 of them, we didn't have enough vehicles to make sure they were comfortable. The trailer had a bar that ran along the floor, normally used as a tie-down for cargo. We placed some blankets down, then wrapped the cuffs around the bar. I know it sounds pretty cruel, but no one wanted the prisoners rushing us when we opened the door. It was for our protection as much as theirs. We cut some holes in the ceiling of the trailer so they could have light and fresh air. We weren't overly cruel.

Liet was the only one who wasn't riding in the back. He would have, but he insisted on acting like a child, kicking and screaming and calling us all the names he could think of. Eventually, we just had to drug him, give him some sleeping pills to get him to shut up. If the prison system and government had still been up and running, our actions would have been viewed as cruelty. Lucky for us, the government was long gone, and they didn't have to deal with Liet. We didn't beat him, just drugged him. You have no idea how much more pleasant it was with him unconscious. It was almost heavenly. From there, we laid him in the sleeper cab.

Quinn and I drove the truck with the prisoners, while Pam and Tanya took a fuel tanker. Poor Tanya. She looked like she was going to lose it. Not only was she still mourning the loss of her father, she was forced to head into the West. The cesspool of zombie creation. She only knew what The Families told her about the place, that she would die instantly out there. She wore her fear on her pale face. I grabbed her arm before she climbed into the cab of the truck.

"I know it doesn't mean much, but you will be just fine out there."

She swallowed thickly and nodded. "I'm sure I will. I'll have you guys to back me up." She tried to force a smile.

"It's bad, but it's not as bad as they told you it is." I thought back to Quinn and I's first trip out, how he tried to make me feel better. "As long as you use your head, you'll survive." I handed her a silver 1911. "This helps, too."

She took the gun and stared at it for a while. I was about to turn and head to my truck when her voice stopped me.

"I'm sorry I blamed the zombie attack on you."

I turned back to her. "It's all right. I completely understand why you would think that."

She looked up, her eyes red-rimmed, tears threatened to fall. "No, it's not all right. You've been nothing but nice to me. You trusted me when you didn't have to. I've always been mean to you. From the beginning. You were so strong, so confident. I was scared. Always scared." She lowered her gaze. "I hated myself for that. For not being able to wonder about the zombies. For not wanting to." She looked up, and a tear found its way down her cheek. "When you came back, I thought, 'This is my chance. Now I can do something.' But in the back of my brain, I didn't want to act. I still wanted to pretend like the zombies didn't exist. That's why I blamed you. It all became too real."

I placed a hand on her shoulder and took a deep breath. I wanted to tell her it was all right, that things were going to be fine, but the words caught in my throat. I didn't know if things were going to be all right. I didn't even know if Kyle and Bill were still alive. Plus, I was kind of angry at her for her cowardice. I couldn't tell her that, and I wouldn't, but she did mess things up a little.

"We'll fix it, don't worry." It was the only thing that would come out of my mouth. I patted her shoulder and headed to the passenger seat of my semi. Tanya climbed into her seat. The door closed behind me as I walked away.

Quinn glanced at me as I stepped into the truck. "You all right?" Concern covered his face.

I nodded. "Yeah. I'm fine. Sorry. I've got a lot on my mind." I nodded toward the back. "How's our prisoner doing?"

"Sleeping soundly."

"Good. Let's hope he stays that way."

Quinn put the truck in gear, and we rolled down the highway. As we passed through the abandoned guard towers, I couldn't help but think how much better the world was going to be once North Platte was gone. Maybe it would actually force The Families into action. Of course, we weren't exactly sure Florida was going to attack us, we were being cautious.

Three miles outside of town, we ran into a zombie horde. With a smile on his lips, Quinn pushed the pedal to the floor. I rolled my eyes, but couldn't stop the smile from curling onto my lips. The creatures thumped against the front of the truck, a couple hands and a few arms flew over the top. Blood and ooze coated the hood, a few drops landed on the windshield. Quinn sprayed the ichor off with wiper fluid. He looked at me.

"This is so much more fun when you don't have to get out to clean it up. I hope we always have people around who want to wash trucks."

"Yeah, it's not without its charm." I smiled back.

As we smiled at each other, something large flew over the hood and slammed into the glass. A loud popping resounded through the cab. Instinctively, I threw up my good arm to protect my face, and Quinn slammed on the brakes. He pulled over onto the side of the road. Panting, with my heart beating a million miles a minute, I glanced at him.

"What was that?"

He stared out the windshield. "I don't know, but it took a nice chuck out of the glass."

I looked at where he indicated and noticed a divot.

"You can still drive it, right?"

The walkie talkie I had on my belt clicked with static, followed by Pam's voice.

"You guys all right up there?"

I pulled it off my belt and pushed the button. "Yeah, we're fine. We're heading out again."

Why hadn't we used the walkies before? We could have called Bill and Kyle for backup in many situations. Oh, well. Live and learn.

I signaled for Quinn to move, then heard something in the distance. It was a sound I knew I had heard somewhere before, but it had been so long, I couldn't place it. Quinn put the truck in gear and pushed on the gas, drowning out the noise. I grabbed his arm.

"Shhh!"

He stared at me. "What?"

"The truck. Turn it off."

He did as I instructed, and the sound got louder. I cocked my head to the side and closed my eyes, trying to place that noise. The walkie talkie crackled again.

"What's going on now?" Pam asked.

I put the speaker up to my mouth. "Do you hear that thumping noise?"

It was silent for a moment. "I do. It sounds like it's behind us."

I rolled down my window and poked my head out. My gaze focused on North Platte. There were two black dots on the horizon. My mouth dropped open.

"Oh, my god," I whispered.

The helicopters hovered over the courthouse for a few seconds before the doors on the side flew open and guards with rocket launchers shot their missiles into the town. Flames erupted with a loud whoosh. They circled the buildings and fired until every last one of them was ablaze.

My heart leapt into my throat. I couldn't tear my eyes away from the destruction. At least we knew the answer to our question, it was no longer speculation if Florida was going to wipe us off the map.

The choppers finished their circle of the city, which took a few minutes, then headed down the highway toward us. My stomach knotted as they flew over, and I pulled my head back into the cab. Without having to say a word, Quinn started the engine and put the truck into gear. We flew down the road. I kept my eyes on the helicopters in the rearview. If they had wanted, they could have followed us, blown us right off the road. I assumed that since they didn't, they didn't have any ammo left. But that didn't make me feel better. They knew we left. It wouldn't take them long to figure out they didn't kill anyone in the city. It was only a matter of time before they hunted us. The color drained out of my face, my skin felt prickly and hot. I gazed at Quinn. He was as white as I imagined I was.

"They have helicopters." It was the only thing I could manage out of my mouth. "They have freaking helicopters!"

"I know," he replied. "This changes the game." He glanced at me over his shoulder. "We're screwed."

Death To The Undead

CHAPTER 4

We drove around for 4 hours, taking back roads and doubling back on ourselves, just to make sure the helicopters weren't following us. I kept checking the rearview, but I couldn't see anything. The last thing we wanted was for Florida to know where we moved to. They blew North Platte up from the sky, what would stop them from doing that to Dashton?

I was still in shock, still not truly believing what I had seen. Helicopters? It had been years since anything was in the sky. I shouldn't have been surprised. After all, they did have TV and radio in Florida, along with running water and reliable electricity. Nothing for them had changed; they were still living in luxury. They didn't have to waste time on surviving and fighting off zombies, they could focus on keeping their technology running. That was aggravating. They wasted so much valuable time. They could use those resources to fry the undead from the sky. The battle against the walking dead could be taken care of in months. But no, they were too concerned with power and control. They had to hoard their weapons. What jerks.

Again, it was something that probably shouldn't have surprised me. Back in the day, I used to study and be fascinated with that type of behavior. I wanted to talk to the people who dominated others, figure out why they did it. I still wanted to know why, but there were more pressing matters at hand. Survival being at the top of my list.

The squeak of the brakes and the jerk of the semi as it slowed brought me out of my thoughts. I glanced out the window. Quinn stopped in a tunnel that had been carved through the mountain. We would be safe from sight as long as the helicopters didn't hover at either end. Either way, it gave us a chance to figure things out.

I stared at him. He sat with his hands folded in his lap, his lips pursed, his gaze meeting mine.

"We've got to warn the others," he stated.

I nodded. "For sure."

"And not just the people from North Platte. Remember those survivors we found in the mall in Casper?"

I searched my memory. "I do. They were the ones with the mini gun, right?"

"Yeah. Those guys. If the copters head there, they might think they've found us and blow them off the map."

I hadn't thought about that. In fact, I hadn't thought about the other survivors since we left. I was so focused on taking down Liet, everything else took a back seat. But Quinn was right, we had to warn them. We had to give them a fighting chance. Maybe it would be enough for them to join up with us, help us take down Florida. It was probably wishful thinking, but I didn't have anything else.

I nodded again. "We do. We need to warn them. Let's take care of him first," I jerked my head toward the sleeper cabin, "then we can warn the others."

Quinn put the truck in gear. "Sounds like a plan."

Death To The Undead

I pulled out my walkie talkie and told Pam and Tanya what we were going to do.

***

Dashton was situated high in the mountains, much higher than I expected. The road was narrow and faded. Obviously, no one had been there in a long time. There were fresh marks from the convoy from North Platte, but otherwise it looked abandoned. The town was nestled in a natural bowl in the mountain, a place that had been carved out by glacial erosion. It was surrounded on two sides by the forest. One side was a steep granite cliff that led to the top of the mountain, and the other side was a sheer drop off. The main road was the easiest way in, but it wasn't the only way. The other routes would have been tricky and required skill, like rock-climbing knowledge. More power to anyone who tried to get in that way. They were treacherous.

The town itself was a cluster of five buildings, the majority of which had been partially knocked down by the weather. It was a textbook example of a ghost town. The convoy parked in the center of town, if you could call it that, and made shelter as best as they could in the ruins. They set up tarps and tents to protect them from the howling wind, but it was a losing battle. Winter was right around the corner. How were we going to make it? Yeah, the town was hidden from the rest of the world, even the helicopters would be hard-pressed to find us, but we weren't going to survive the elements. I trusted Quinn, though. He knew what he was doing. He had to.

We pulled into town and jumped down from the cab. Several inhabitants approached us, trying not to complain about the situation but wondering what was going on. Quinn placed his hands in his back pockets and spit on the ground before speaking. A smile spread across his lips, it irritated some of the others.

"I guess I forgot to tell you the best part about Dashton."

He walked to a decrepit building built next to the mountain face. He pulled open the door and it clattered onto the ground. A crowd formed around him, arms crossed over their chests and eyebrows furrowed. I stood right next him, trying to figure out what he was doing. He stepped across the small room to the wall at the back. With a fist, he pounded on the gray wood. It fell over with a creak, stirring up a cloud of dust as it slammed onto the floor. I blinked to get the dirt out of my eyes, then noticed the opening in the rock. I smiled. I knew exactly where it led. It was just like Quinn's house. There were tunnels and rooms scattered throughout the mountain. Not only would it be relief from the elements, but it would be definite protection from Florida and the zombies. I looked at the crowd. Their mouths hung open in shock.

"We can work on getting the buildings habitable until the snow comes. The caves will be a temporary home until that is done." He nodded into the darkness. "I doubt there's anything in there, but we'd better do a sweep just in case. You have your flashlight?"

I grabbed the flashlight off my belt, and I pulled the gun out of the holster on my hip. Six of us headed in. Several others wanted to go, but we didn't want too many people in there. It was going to be dark, sounds were going to echo, and no one wanted to get accidentally shot. Having the other four in there with us made me nervous enough, I didn't know how itchy of trigger fingers they had. I knew how to clear an area with Quinn, and I knew he wouldn't shoot me. But he insisted. The network of caves was large with several tunnels and offshoots; we needed several people to watch our backs. What other choice did I have? I relented.

I took a deep breath and stepped into the cave. The air was cool, and dripping water echoed through the space. Our flashlight beams bounced off the black walls. I couldn't imagine there were any zombies in the cave. How would they have gotten so far up the mountain? There wasn't a food source around. I imagined one of the people behind me being overly skittish, jumping at every sound and accidentally shooting one of us. I glanced over my shoulder, just in case.

As we proceeded into the cave, it opened up into a huge room. Seriously, we could have parked three semis in there and stacked two on top of each other. There were several other caves that led off in different directions. As I shone the light around, I counted six. I also noticed some markings on the walls, blue and red triangles. They were faded, but I knew someone put them there. We congregated in the middle of the room, forming a circle per Quinn's instructions.

"Some of these tunnels go for miles," he whispered, "but they come out next to towns and cities. It's possible a zombie could have fallen in and is wandering around. You need to remain vigilant and keep your eyes and ears open. The tunnels marked with blue triangles lead to different chambers, rooms with no outlets. The ones marked with red triangles lead out. There are three that lead out. We will head down in teams of two. Check your targets before firing. After you've finished your search and headed back, go outside. You don't need to hang out in the cave. We don't need anyone getting shot. Understand?"

He shined his light in each of our faces and we nodded our understanding. Quinn then proceeded to give us each our assignment. Naturally, we were together. I looked forward to being in the dark with him. It had been a while since we had the opportunity to be alone. Keeping the survivors of North Platte happy and making sure they were working was a full-time job. I knew exactly why Liet was so stressed out all the time.

As we stepped into the tunnel, the walls narrowed and the ceiling got lower. If I stretched my arms out to the side, my elbows slightly bent, I could touch both walls. I could barely touch the ceiling with my head by standing on my tiptoes.

Death To The Undead

For whatever reason, Quinn insisted on going in before me. I think it was some type of chivalric display, which was flattering, but I could take care of myself. However, since I didn't think we were going to run into any zombies, I didn't mind being at the back. It gave me a chance to relax a little. When we were 15 steps into the cave, I grabbed the back of his shirt. He spun around quickly, shining his light into my eyes.

"What?" he hissed. "What's wrong?"

I pushed the beam out of my face as I holstered my gun, stepping closer to Quinn. I wrapped my arm around his neck.

"Nothing," I said in the sexiest whisper I could muster. "I just thought we could spend a little alone time."

I saw the smile on his face before he wrapped his arms around my waist and directed the light behind me. His lips connected with mine, and we kissed in the dark for a while. I wished the moment wouldn't end. I liked being with him, feeling his lips and the heat from his body. I liked not having to worry about zombies or helicopters or crazy families from Florida. I was just about to lose myself in the moment, to let all my guards down and relax, when a hissing sound echoed through the cave. We pulled away at the same time. We still held onto each other, but our heads were cocked to opposite sides, listening.

The hiss sounded again, a long release of air with a slight whistle to it, as if coming from between someone's teeth. It was followed by a rock clunking onto the floor and a shuffling sound. Quinn turned and shone the flashlight down the hall. I directed my light back the way we came, hoping it was just one of the others who had gotten lost. Unfortunately, I didn't see anything. I stepped back so I was in contact with Quinn and pulled my gun out.

"Do you see anything?" I asked over my shoulder.

"No. But let's keep moving forward."

I turned and placed my hand on the small of his back, my head bent to the side so I could see around his body. The hiss sounded again, followed by the shuffling, then was followed by a grunt and a click. Was it an animal? It had to be. There was no way a zombie could get in here. No way. We continued forward.

The cave narrowed and turned to the right. Quinn pressed himself against the wall and shone his light around the corner. I couldn't see what was there, but from the way he jerked his light back, I knew it wasn't good. He illuminated himself and signaled for me to press against the wall. Scowling, I did as I was told, and he moved around the corner. The crack of the gun was deafening. Instantly, my ears rang and felt numb. I opened and closed my jaw, hoping the motion would help me hear again. It didn't work. Quinn grabbed my arm and pulled me around the wall.

I saw something in his beam, what looked like a human crumpled on the ground. As we drew closer, Quinn slowed. He shone his light down the tunnel before toeing the corpse in front of us. It didn't move, so he stepped over it. I lingered, shining my light on the body. It was a woman, with long black hair that hung in greasy clumps. Her face was ashen, her cheeks sunken in. Her lips were pulled back, making it appear as if she had a permanent snarl. She wore a dark gray suit and purple shirt. The clothes weren't all that tattered, just a little dirty with a few tears, and all of the exposed skin seemed to be intact. She hadn't been undead for long. The bullet hole entered just below her left eye, discontinuing her endless and pointless walk on the earth. I stepped over her and followed Quinn.

We continued through to the end of the tunnel. It took us forever. Wandering around in the dark with no way to look at your watch or figure out how far you've walked is a bit disconcerting. I thought for sure we'd be trapped in the mountain for the rest of our lives. I was just about to open my mouth and say something when I felt a cool breeze. The tunnel also seemed to get lighter. I had my hand on the small of Quinn's back, and I pushed up to my tiptoes, hoping to look over his shoulder.

"Hey, calm down," he called to me. "I don't want to rush out there without knowing what we're getting into."

I lowered myself, not realizing I had been pushing on him. "Sorry."

He continued walking.

When we were close to the opening, we slowed and pressed our backs against the wall. We made our way cautiously to the entrance. My shoulder hit a couple of protruding rocks, sending waves of pain through my back. I winced. I hated that I still wore a sling. I hated that I would be in one for several more weeks. I cursed Liet in my mind. I wouldn't have been in the situation if it weren't for him. I shook my head, an attempt to clear the thoughts. We had a job to do, and thinking about the past wouldn't help. We continued through the tunnel.

We reached the end, and Quinn signaled for me to say back. He poked his head around both sides of the opening, taking in the area. From my vantage point, I could see pine trees and nothing else. He jerked his head to the side, and we stepped into the fresh air. The ground was mostly level. I don't know why, but I half expected to walk out onto a thin ledge, the mountain falling away beneath us. I figured we would have to carefully shimmy our way to the side, praying and hoping we didn't slip into oblivion. However, with the forest stretched out before us, it made a lot more sense of how the zombie would have gotten into the cave. We took a few steps further into the trees.

A bird twittered overhead, followed by a flap of wings. A squirrel chattered in the distance, and a twig snapped. None of it concerned me, but I kept a vigilant eye out. It was too easy for things to sneak up on you in the trees. I was under the impression that the zombie was a fluke occurrence. I didn't see any towns or habitations, so how did it get into the cave? More birds flew over, tweeting as if everything was normal. I lowered my gun and removed my hand from Quinn's back. He took a couple more steps, then stopped, turning to face me. He glanced at something over my shoulder. His eyes went wide and his jaw dropped open.

It was one of the moments from a horror film. From his reaction, I knew I didn't want to turn around, but I also wanted to face my attacker. I hoped it was a bear. Please let it be a bear. I turned. Right next to the tunnel opening was another zombie. This one was an older man, his hair gray, his black dress pants shredded to the knee. Half of his white, button-up shirt was untucked, the rest of it covered in dirt. Like the woman in the cave, his skin was pretty much intact, except for the chunk that had been ripped out of his neck. He turned his glassy eyes toward us, his mouth opened. Before he could moan, I raised my gun and shot. The bullet tore through his jaw, exploding his head on the rocks behind him. His body crumpled to the ground. I looked at Quinn.

"Where are they coming from?"

He shook his head and scanned the trees. "I don't know. There has to be some kind of town around here. Unfortunately, we don't have time to find it right now." He gestured with his eyes toward the sky. "The sun will be going down in a few hours, and we need to block this opening. We don't want anything surprising us in the middle of the night."

I glanced from him to the cave to the trees. My throat felt tight. I still couldn't understand why there were zombies that far up the mountain. And why did they look so fresh? Most of the zombies we ran into had been turned years ago. Their clothes were extremely tattered and decomposition was setting in. These ones looked like they had only been wandering for months. Maybe I was wrong. Maybe the cool mountain air kept them preserved. God, I hoped the cool mountain preserved them.

"Why don't we just do a sweep? See if we can find their source. We still have a few hours."

He shook his head. "We don't know how long it's going to take or how many there are. There's only two of us, and you're wounded. I think it's best if I get some of the guys to help me block off this opening, then they can do a search while we head to Casper."

I sighed. Of course he was right. I forgot about warning the people in Casper. We needed to get to them as soon as possible. We had no idea when Florida would do their patrols. The sooner we got to them, the better.

"You're right. Let's head back." I headed toward the cave. I stopped right before stepping into the darkness and stared at Quinn. "You know this isn't going to sit well with them. You know they're going to freak."

Quinn took a deep breath and spit. "Yeah, I know. But they knew the risks coming out here."

I clicked my tongue. "Like they had a choice."

He placed his hand on my shoulder. "They always had a choice. Unfortunately, it was between being killed by people from Florida or zombies. The best thing we can do is try to keep this as quiet as possible. We'll tell a few people, those we can trust. We don't need to cause a panic."

Again, he was right. We were in a tough spot. At least this way they had a fighting chance. At least out here they could see the threat coming at them and have a chance to defend themselves. I moved so I was next to Quinn, resting my head on his shoulder.

"I guess we better stop wasting time."

He kissed the top of my head before we made our way back through the tunnel.

CHAPTER 5

Two hours after sunset, Quinn and the others came back. He made it a point to speak to Lydia, Chester, and Pam, and they were more than willing to help block the cave entrance. They kept it quiet so it wouldn't scare anyone. If anyone did ask, we told them the tunnel wasn't safe, that rocks were falling, so we closed it off so no one would get hurt. It was sufficient.

The other groups who ventured into the cave with us waited outside when we walked out. Luckily, none of them ran into any trouble. Once Quinn gave the okay, several families and individuals moved their stuff into the mountain. Others stayed outside. The wind died down once the sun set, and even though the air was cool, it was pleasant. We had to keep the prisoners in the back of the truck. There was nowhere else to place them. They grumbled and were upset about it, but what did we care? They made their choice. At least they were dry and protected. We made them dinner and gave them blankets. It was more than they could expect in a third-world country.

We had to cuff Liet to a handle in the semi. Again, there was nothing to do with him. There weren't any cells to put him in, and he couldn't be around the general population. We were afraid of what he'd do and what others would do to him. We gave him more sleeping pills, too, just to keep him under control. I felt a little bad about doing it, wondering if we were doing some long-term damage, but then my shoulder started aching again, and I wanted to shove the whole bottle down his throat. I refrained, of course.

I sat next to the fire, lounging on a blanket and staring into the flames. After whacking my arm on the rocks in the cave, my shoulder throbbed, so I took some pain pills. They numbed me out, not just my shoulder, my entire body. It was divine. I didn't worry about zombies or helicopters or Liet. I just watched the blues, whites, and oranges dance in the fire.

Quinn sat next to me and kissed my cheek. I turned my head to look at him, smiling. Concern covered his face.

"You all right?"

"Yeah. Why wouldn't I be?"

He pointed to my face. "Your eyes look a little glazed. Did you take something?"

I nodded and focused my gaze back on the flames. "Yeah. My shoulder was killing me. I took a pain pill."

"What did you take?"

I shrugged. "I don't know. Something out of the First Aid kit Bill carried around."

Quinn placed his hand on my leg and sighed. "We've got to figure out how to get the brothers out of there."

I placed my head on his shoulder, suddenly overcome by intense sadness. "I know. Do you think they're all right? Do you think The Families did anything to them? Like tortured them?"

Visions of Bill and Kyle tied to a table ran through my head. I saw Mrs. Johnson hooking up electrodes to their chests and heads, plugging it into a battery, and laughing manically as she flipped the switch. I squeezed my eyes shut, attempting to get rid of the image.

Quinn picked up a stick and poked at the logs in the fire. "Nah. I'm sure they're fine. Why would they need to torture them? They have no idea we were planning an attack. They don't even know who they are. For all they know, Bill and Kyle are just two drifters who snuck into their state."

I hoped he was right. It was impossible to know what Tanya told them. She said she didn't mention anything about the invasion, but maybe she said that for her own safety. She didn't know what we would do to her. She didn't know if we would get angry and kill her. But then again, maybe she didn't care. Maybe she was hoping we would kill her. She just lost her dad, her last living relative. What else did she have to lose?

I glanced across the fire to where she sat. She was staring into the flames just like me. It reminded me of that night my mom and I spent in the lookout tower, the night after the explosion at the base. I remembered wishing and hoping Dad was going to come back. I remembered needing Mom to say something, to comfort me, but it didn't happen. She was lost in her sorrow, tormented by the thought that Dad was gone.

Death To The Undead

I wondered what Tanya thought. She hadn't said much since we left North Platte. In fact, I almost forgot she was there. She drifted around the camp, lost in her own mind, her head down while she chewed on her nail. If anyone asked her anything, she would respond with a short answer, sometimes the reply bordered on incoherent. It was sad. I knew she was depressed, trying to figure out what to do next, and I hoped she figured it out soon. She was strong and another human, we needed her help.

"There's something down there." Quinn's voice was soft, whispered close to my ear.

I tore my gaze from Tanya and turned to look at him. "Where?"

"Down the hill from where we killed the zombies. I did a quick reconnaissance, and I saw a chain link fence and some buildings. They're hidden in the trees. I think after we warn the people in Casper, before we head to Florida, we need to check it out."

"What are we going to do about Florida?"

"I don't know, Krista. I just don't know. We need to give it a little time, though. Let things settle down. They're expecting an attack now, some type of retaliation. We need to draw it out, let things calm down, then we'll make our move."

I was so glad he didn't say anything about attacking Florida at the same time as North Platte. That drove me crazy. We both knew that was the best plan, but it wouldn't have worked. First of all, we didn't have enough people.

Secondly, the workers in Nebraska wouldn't have been able to hold out long enough. If we hadn't done something, they might have taken Liet out on their own. Where would that have left us? I wasn't looking for glory or recognition, but there was a personal vendetta against Liet I needed to fulfill. I knew the workers were more than capable of fending for themselves, but Quinn and I knew the West. However, they might have made it without us.

Maybe I looked at it from the wrong perspective. Maybe we should have let them stage their own coup. I'm sure they would have eventually. They were being pushed to the breaking point. Then, I wouldn't have gotten shot, and Quinn and I could've disappeared at his ranch. We would be worry and stress free. But no one else would. I mentally shrugged. What did it matter? Things had already happened, and I couldn't change the situation.

A pounding resounded in the distance. I lifted my head slightly and glanced over the fire toward the semis. It sounded like someone slammed a door. Someone probably forgot something in the truck, so I laid my head back down and attempted to get comfortable. Then, it happened again. A little louder.

"Is someone playing in the trucks?" I asked Quinn.

I looked at him. He stared toward the trucks, too. His squinted into the darkness.

The pounding sounded twice more, followed by a metal on metal scrape.

Quinn jumped from his seat, dropping me onto my side.

Death To The Undead

"Oh, crap! I think that's the truck Liet is in."

I scrambled to my feet as Quinn ran ahead. As I came around the front of the semi, the driver's side door was open. Quinn was inside, glancing into the sleeper cabin. He pulled his gun out of the holster and jumped from the cab.

"I need backup!" he yelled.

My heart skipped a beat, my throat tightened. This couldn't be happening. How would he have gotten out? He was drugged with sleeping pills. He was cuffed to a bar on the inside. The door was locked. I willed myself to fly, hoping I was in a pain-pill-induced dream. Nothing. My feet remained planted on the ground. I wasn't dreaming.

Several others surrounded us, their hands on their hips, wondering what was going on. Quinn grabbed his flashlight off his belt. He clicked it on and illuminated the ground. Footprints led away from the truck, into the trees, and Quinn followed after them.

"What's going on?" Pam wondered. She stood right next to me.

"Liet got out." The words caught in my throat. I had to choke them out, unable and unwilling to believe I had to say them.

Without a word, Pam disappeared behind me. She re-emerged a few seconds later with a rife and another flashlight. She took off after Quinn. I didn't know what to do. I stood next to the truck, my mouth hanging open. The pills dulled my senses, made it hard to think, so my reactions were slow. I couldn't just stand there. I had to help. I moved to take off after them, but someone grabbed my arm. I turned to see Tanya.

"What are you doing?" she asked.

"I...I have to find him. We can't let him go."

She released her grip and nodded toward my sling. "You can't go into the woods with your arm like that. The ground is uneven, what happens if you trip?"

"I'll be fine."

"No, you won't. You need to leave it to them."

Lydia and Chester approached at that moment, wondering what happened. Tanya explained the situation, and they turned to the others. They organized a group and headed into the woods after Pam and Quinn. Tanya led me back to the fire and sat me down. If I had full control of my senses, I would have protested. I would have jerked out her grasp and headed into the trees. I knew it wasn't a good idea. I would be useless, but I loathed not being able to help. I hated waiting for news. But she was right. I wouldn't be any help. If Liet sensed my weakness, he could use me against the others. What if he took me hostage? What if he took the opportunity to kill me? Quinn, Pam, and the others were more than capable, they could handle it. They had to.

I didn't sleep. I was tired, but I had to know what happened to Liet. I sat by the fire, staring into the darkness, waiting for them to come back. It was going to be at any moment. He didn't get far, he couldn't. The sleeping pills slowed him down.

Death To The Undead

The group didn't return until day break. I stood and waited for Quinn to approach. His face was gray, his eyes pink from lack of sleep. His mouth turned down in a frown, his shoulders slumped forward. Pam walked behind him. She didn't look much better. They plopped on the ground in front of me. Tanya threw some more logs onto the fire. I moved in front of Quinn. Kneeling in front of him, I placed my hand on his knee.

"What happened? Did you get him?"

He clenched his jaw. "No. He's gone."

I swallowed thickly. It felt like someone punched me in the stomach. I couldn't catch my breath. I fell onto my butt and placed a hand on my forehead. How could he have gotten away? We took so many precautions. It was my worst nightmare. The only thing I could hope for was that the zombies would take care of him. He was unarmed, and we were a long way from civilization. I knew it was desperate, I knew Liet was a survivor and would probably make it through, but I had to tell myself something.

"We've posted guards," Pam explained. "And we'll fortify the camp while you're gone. He won't be able to come back around here without someone knowing." She leaned forward and lowered her voice. "Just so you know, if he does come back around here, I'm not taking him alive. And I doubt anyone else is going to either."

I nodded. It had to be done. No one could fault them for thinking like that. Or blame them if they went through with it. We kept him alive as a prisoner so the history books would portray us as being fair and perfect role models for democracy. All bets went out the window after his escape. He was dangerous, and no one knew what he was going to do. I glanced at Quinn. If anyone was going to have any issues, it was him. He just looked at Pam, quickly nodded his head, then went back to staring at the fire.

"Do you think he'll come back?" Tanya asked.

We all looked at her.

"It's hard to say," Pam answered. "If Liet thinks he can benefit in some way by coming back, he will. It's also possible he'll try to make it to Florida. Inform them of our plans and get back up to wipe us off the planet. He knows where we are."

Tanya's face paled. "But that will take him a while, right? I mean, he doesn't have a car. And there are zombies out there. He could get killed."

Quinn sighed, drawing our attention to him.

"He could die and he could make it to Florida." He folded his arms over his chest. "Liet's smart enough to know how to avoid danger. He's also smart enough to know he needs weapons, so he'll find the closest town he can. We have to assume the worst."

Tanya pointed toward the woods. "Then, you have to find him. You have to hunt him down like a dog and kill him."

"That's what he's counting on," I spoke softly.

Tanya stared at me, wide eyed. "What do you mean?"

"He wants us to go after him. That gives him time to head to Florida, and it takes us away from planning the attack. If we're busy looking for him, we can't cause any more damage."

She scrunched up her nose, stood up, and paced. "You should have killed him when you got the chance. Then, none of this would have happened."

"Is that what you would have done?" Quinn's voice was low, almost inaudible.

Tanya stopped moving and stared at him over the flames. "That is exactly what I would have done." She threw her arms out to the side, gesturing to the camp. "Look how many people you just put in danger."

"And what if we needed information from him? What if he had some great secret that would help us take The Families down?"

She huffed. "Like he'd give it to you."

Quinn stared at her for a moment. A hard stare. His jaw muscles tightened. "He definitely wouldn't be able to tell us if he were dead."

She huffed again. "If he were dead, your problem would be solved. All of these people would be safe."

"What problem is that, Tanya? Would the zombies be taken care of? Would we have freed the people in Florida? If you ask me, you're prone to snap decisions. You don't think about the consequences. That's why you were so quick to blame us for the zombies in the back of the truck and to let Bill and Kyle get arrested. You couldn't think up a lie to protect the brothers? Did you ever think maybe they had some answers?"

Her eyes grew wide and she stopped pacing. "To what? They weren't there when the truck came, how would they know if you placed the zombies or not?"

Quinn shook his head. "They know us better than that. They would have vouched for us. The world doesn't revolve around you and your pain, Tanya. There are bigger things out there, more people who counted on them. You jumped to a conclusion, and out of anger and spite, you did what you thought was right. We could've done the same thing. We could've killed Liet out of anger, but where would that leave us? With blood on our hands. With the guilt of knowing we killed a human being. He might have had a change of heart, he might have decided he wanted to help us, but we'd never know if we killed him. Just like you'll never know what Bill and Kyle could have done for the revolution because you let them get captured."

He continued to stare at her, his face turned red. Her anger softened, and her eyes became glassy. She plopped onto the ground, her chin quivered. I thought at any moment the tears would fall. I wanted to say something, I wanted to break the tension, but I didn't know how. Tanya did what she thought was right. Yes, it was out of anger, but how was she supposed to know? Did she jeopardize the mission and the lives of our friends? Yes, but it was done. We couldn't change it. I was shocked about Quinn's reaction to it. He'd been so cool before, so calm. The hate seared in his tone.

He did his best to keep it under control, but we all heard it. It was a little scary.

Tanya took a deep breath and turned away. Quinn lowered his gaze to the fire. He poked at it with his stick. I glanced at Pam. She shrugged, then turned away. What could anyone say? The stress was getting out of hand. It was one thing to plan an invasion. It was another to figure out how to free your friends. It was a completely different ball game when your archenemy escaped. We didn't know what he planned. We could only hope he would try to make it to Florida and die in the process. Was it the nicest thing to hope for? Of course not. But it would be a lot more merciful than what would happen if he came back to the camp.

Abruptly, Quinn stood from the fire. "We need to head to Casper. We need to warn those people."

I wasn't going to argue. Anything was better than sitting in that tension. I stood, and so did Pam.

"You want a lookout?" she asked.

Quinn faced her. The anger melted from his face. His jaw muscles loosened. "I do, but someone needs to stay here in case Liet comes back. You have the respect of the people, you can keep them together. Krista and I can handle it."

She nodded.

We headed to the semi Liet escaped from. After detaching the trailer, we drove down the mountain. I stared out the window, still searching for something to say to

Quinn. Nothing came to mind. It had been a long night, and we were both tired. It would have been best to get some sleep, but we didn't have time. We wasted enough of it looking for Liet, we had to make sure those people in Casper were going to be safe.

I placed my elbow on the door handle and leaned my forehead against my hand. Everything was unraveling. Everything seemed so bleak. There were zombies close to the safe haven we led the survivors of North Platte to. If even one of those things got into camp and bit one person, it was over. Even if they stopped the threat, Quinn and I were done. No one would trust us, and they would probably blame us for not warning them. Florida was on the warpath and had the people, weapons, and technology to take us down. Liet escaped. I knew he wouldn't rest until he made Quinn and I pay. I didn't even want to think about what he was going to do to us. I didn't say it out loud, but Quinn was right. We should have attacked North Platte and Florida at the same time.

CHAPTER 6

A bump caused my head to hit the window, and I jerked awake. I hadn't realized I fell asleep. I stretched and glanced over at Quinn. His eyes were focused on the road, his jaw muscles still prominent. He was still upset, still thinking about what happened in Dashton. Again, I tried to think of something to say. Still, nothing came to mind. I glanced out the windshield. Casper lay stretched out in front of us. A horde of zombies milled on the horizon. I thought back to the last time we were at the mall. Hundreds of them had converged on our position, ready to attack and eat anything that ventured into the parking lot. Luckily, the survivors in the mall were prepared for such an occasion. I could still smell the blood and feel the slick gore as we hurried across the parking lot. The gun made quick work of their rotting flesh. I wondered if it was possible to mount a mini gun on a semi. Then, someone could ride on top and just fire at will. Maybe it was something we could contemplate when we started killing off zombies.

Quinn pulled onto the exit that would take us to the mall. My stomach fluttered. The people weren't very happy the last time we happened onto their sanctuary, I could only imagine what they were going to say when we pulled up again. Would they believe us when we told them about the helicopters? Would they be willing to leave?

"What do you think they'll say?" I turned to look at Quinn.

He blinked and shook his head. "I don't know." He looked at me. "We have to try, though."

"I know." I cleared my throat and wiped my sweaty hand on my pants. "Even if they don't believe us, if the helicopters do show up, they'll know what to do."

He nodded but didn't say anything.

We pulled into the parking lot. Six zombies milled around, obliviously walking in circles, waiting for prey to chance by. They would be easy to take care of. I could still see the mess from our last visit. The asphalt was stained an unnatural brown. Chunks of flesh and body parts had been dried by the sun, they were shriveled and wrinkled, the skin colored like tanned leather. The smell of rotting flesh faded, but was still present. It drifted into the cab. I gagged. Quinn shut off the engine, staring at the building.

"How do you want to do this?"

He leaned forward. "I say we take care of the zombies from the truck. Fire out the windows. Then, we walk in again, just like we did last time." He glanced at me.

"Okay. Sounds like a plan."

He reached for his door handle.

"I'm sure you were right," I blurted out. I didn't know where the words came from, and I didn't know why I picked that particular moment to say them, but they had to come out.

He froze, his forehead wrinkled. "About what?"

"About Bill and Kyle. I'm sure The Families haven't hurt them."

Death To The Undead

He sighed. "I wish I could be so sure."

I stretched across the seats and wrapped my arm around his neck. His arm encircled my waist. I knew he was worried about them. I knew when he said that at camp, it was more for his benefit and not mine. I could tell when he confronted Tanya, the rage burning in his eyes, that he didn't know what happened to them. He was great about keeping his emotions in check, which was needed when we had a job to do, but he also had emotions, and they always found a way to the surface.

He buried his head in my shoulder. I stroked the back of his hair. We sat like that for several moments. Eventually, he lifted his head but didn't pull away. Resting his forehead against mine, he gazed into my eyes.

"We can't worry about them now. They know how to take care of themselves. As much as I want to help them, we have others to help first."

"I know. But you are still entitled to your feelings. If you need to talk about anything, I'm here."

He kissed me. "I know. But we have a job to do."

He turned away and opened his door. I watched him fire a few shots before I rolled down my window and fired at the first creature who wandered into my sights.

The mall seemed more humid than I remembered it. We stood in darkness, shining our flashlights at nothing.

"Hello?" Quinn called. "Anybody here?"

"Maybe they've moved on," I whispered.

"I doubt it. The boards over the windows look new." He took a step further into the room. "Hello?"

I didn't want to remind him about the last time we were here and how hundreds of undead converged on the place. They probably damaged the old boards trying to claw their way in. But I did see his point. If they left, there would be no need to replace them. They could just let the creatures overrun the building. That didn't make me feel better. The leader guy wasn't very happy the last time we were there. In fact, he was down right angry. He wanted to keep his people safe, and who could blame him? How would he react when we told him he might be gunned down by soldiers from Florida? Would he let us leave alive?

"They're probably in another store in the mall. We should check it out." He wandered through the clothes racks.

Taking a deep breath, I followed behind him.

We were about half way through Sears when we heard the shuffling. I immediately froze. I wasn't worried it was a zombie, it didn't sound like one, but I didn't want to be attacked again. They almost killed me the first time, and I had full use of both my arms. I doubted they would take it easy on me just because I was injured. I was still a little bitter about our last meeting in the mall. I didn't realize how much it affected me until I stood in the dark once again. I shone my light around the room, trying to find the person. Even with my injury, if they decided to jump me, I was going to put up one helluva fight. Skulking around in the dark. How fair was that? If I could see them coming, they wouldn't get the upper hand. I thought their actions were cowardly.

"Who's there?" Quinn called. "We don't mean you any harm. We're here to warn you."

"About what?" The rough voice called through the darkness.

It was hard to pinpoint, but it sounded like it came from my right. I shone my light in that direction.

"Show yourself and we'll tell you," I called.

A light clicked on in the distance, and Quinn and I were illuminated in white. We turned to see the source, squinting against the brightness.

"Oh, it's you again," the voice said. "Wait here."

Frozen in the light, we heard the person walk off. I glanced at Quinn, who covered his eyes, trying to see past the light. That didn't sound reassuring. He remembered us, which meant they might be mad at us. I hoped they would let us deliver our warning before threatening to kill us. Or actually murdering us.

More footsteps approached, and the overhead lights clicked on. The spotlight clicked off. With a white blob dancing in front of my eyes, I tried to focus on the group standing in front of us. Their features were a little hard to discern, but I could tell there were about ten of them. The leader, the guy with the graying hair, stepped forward, his hands clasped behind his back. He sighed.

"I thought I told you two never to return."

Quinn held his hands out to his sides. "I know, but we needed to warn you."

The man cleared his throat and tried to hide the agitation in his voice. "About what?"

"Florida has helicopters."

The room was silent for a long time. The man stared at us. I couldn't tell if he was angry or didn't believe us or what. His face showed no emotion. My discomfort grew with each passing second that he didn't speak. If there was a clock in the room, I'm sure I would have heard it ticking. Finally, he sighed and jerked his head to the right.

"Follow me. Let's talk somewhere more comfortable."

We followed the man through the store to the opening that led to the rest of the mall. The chain gate had been opened, and as we passed through, it was pulled shut. It clambered closed with a rattle and the squeak of metal on metal. I cringed. Every zombie within a one-mile radius probably heard that. Not that it mattered; they could take care of them very easily from the roof.

We were led to the old food court. The tables and chairs were still in place, but couches and recliners also lined the area. The survivors made use of the several kitchens in the area, too. I don't know how they did it, but they had the cook tops working, and I could smell their dinner. The scent of bacon and potatoes drifted into my nostrils, followed by something sweet. The unmistakable scent of cookies. I couldn't remember the last time I smelled fresh-baked cookies. It brought back a flood of emotions and memories of my mom. I thought about cold Saturdays mixing the dough while snow fell gently outside the window. I would sneak bites of the uncooked goodness. I didn't care what Mom said, something that tasted that good couldn't have salmonella in it. I was convinced she just told me that because she wanted to hoard the dough for herself. When we baked cookies, the oven made the kitchen so warm and comfortable, like your favorite blanket. The world outside didn't matter. The only worry was making sure the cookies didn't burn. The smell reminded me of happiness and safety.

I inhaled deeply through my nose, savoring the sweetness. My mouth watered and my stomach growled. Because of my exhaustion, I had to fight back bursting into tears. With everything that happened within the past several weeks, my greatest desire was to be back home, to be with my parents, to be safe. It would never happen, I knew that, and it made me sad. Normally, I was able to push the depression deep down. I could force myself to focus on whatever task was at hand, to push the memories aside, but it was getting more and more difficult. There were too many things we had to accomplish, too many tasks that bordered on the impossible, and they seemed to stack up. It was getting to the point where I just wanted to give up. Throw my good hand in the air and let someone else take care of it. I was too young to be burdened with saving the world. And I was tired. So very tired.

Several people were engaged in conversation as we approached, but they stopped and stared at us. I knew their looks were out of curiosity, but it didn't help my mood. I tried to keep my face emotionless, but I wasn't accomplishing it. My face was sour, my anger showing through. How could these people be sitting in here, baking cookies, when the world was going to hell? Why weren't they doing something? Why weren't they taking action? They had the fire power to make a difference, and they were content hiding in the mall. I balled my hand into a fist and clenched my jaw. Don't judge these people until you know their story, I told myself. I took a couple of deep breaths.

The man led us to a collection of couches and chairs at the far end of the dining room. The area was set up just like a living room with a coffee table, end tables, and lamps. They even had magazines on the coffee table. Quinn and I took a seat on the couch, the man sat on a recliner across from us. He sat on the edge, his elbows resting on his knees.

"Now, please tell me exactly why Florida having helicopters should be of concern to me?"

A girl approached and set a tray on the table. It held cookies and mugs of coffee. Quinn and I thanked her, and she walked away. I noticed she wore a new pair of jeans and tank top. We had our share of new clothes, but they didn't stay that way for long. I bit my tongue, keeping comments about being sheltered to myself. We made our decisions, just like they did. I couldn't hold it against them for not knowing an honest day's labor. I'm sure they had their hardships. They just weren't obvious. I picked up a cup of coffee and a cookie.

"We're concerned they might patrol the area, see you and the other survivors, and mistake you for us. We just want to make sure you're going to be safe."

The man leaned back in the chair. He interlaced his fingers, all of them except for his index fingers, and brought them to his lips. He stared at us for a moment.

"I still don't understand what you mean."

Quinn glanced at me. I shrugged one shoulder and focused on my cookie. I bit into it. It was soft, warm, and the chocolate was half melted. It dissolved on my tongue. I closed my eyes, savoring the sweetness. If I died at that moment, I would have been happy. It was the best cookie I ever tasted.

"They might come after you because of what happened in North Platte."

"What happened in North Platte?" the girl who brought us the cookies asked.

"Yes, please enlighten us."

I shoved the rest of the cookie into my mouth, hoping it would choke back the anger that threatened to explode. I chewed slowly; the exertion of the movement brought my emotions under control. It wasn't their fault they didn't know what happened in North Platte. They lived a sheltered life. Communication wasn't what is used to be. How would they know what was going on in the rest of the world? Why would they care? Why would they bother finding out what was happening to other survivors, other humans, as long as they were happy and safe? I fought back every urge in my body to stand from the couch and leave. I wanted to tell them never mind, deal with the situation any way they wanted to. We had enough crap to deal with, we didn't need theirs. But I knew what Quinn would say, and, deep down, I did know staying was the right thing to do. Even if they were sheltered jerks, they still didn't deserve to be blown off the face of the Earth. They deserved a fighting chance.

Quinn calmly told them about Liet and the uprising, but I knew it was a struggle for him. He had his hands folded between his legs, his knuckles were white. He was even more tired than I was. I took a nap in the truck. I imagined how frustrated and irritated he was. I ate another cookie while I waited for him to finish.

When he was done, the man sat quietly, absorbing the information. The girl shifted from one foot to the other, her eyes wide as she stared at him. Without warning, the man slammed his hands onto the arms of the recliner and pushed himself up. I jerked with surprise and almost spilled my coffee.

"Well, we appreciate you taking the time to warn us, but we can take care of ourselves." He gestured with an open hand toward the way we came in.

"Duncan," the girl whispered and stepped forward. She was going to say more, but Duncan held up his hand to silence her.

Death To The Undead

"We have been in this city for a long time now. We keep a vigilant eye. No one will get the upper hand on us."

Quinn stood. "I hope you're right. I really do. They won't think twice about shooting you from the sky."

Duncan's eyes narrowed. "And if it weren't for you and your rebellion, we wouldn't have to worry about that."

By that point, I had enough. I slammed my cookie onto the table before getting to my feet.

"You can't blame us for wanting a better life. We didn't have the luxury in North Platte you have here." I fluttered my hand around the room, indicating the mall.

Duncan stared at me. "We all made our choices. I shouldn't feel sorry or have to pay for the ones you made."

"And what about reclaiming what's ours? What about killing the zombies and taking back America?"

"We're fine where we're at. We don't need anything more."

"Duncan," the girl said again. I heard the disappointment in her voice.

I hoped she would say more, maybe take our side and convince Duncan to do something, but she just walked away.

Quinn huffed. His face turned red, and I knew he was doing everything in his power to stay calm. He opened his mouth to say something, thought better of it, then walked away. I narrowed my eyes and stared at Duncan. I shook my head. There were so many things I could have said to him, so many things I wanted to tell him. I could have given him a speech about taking pride in his nation and wanting a better life for his followers, for his children. I could have told him he would be a hero, that future generations would tell his story for years and years, but I didn't. I didn't waste my breath. Instead, I followed Quinn out of the building.

We sat in the parking lot for a long time. The engine ran, and Quinn stared out the windshield.

"I don't get it. I just don't get." He didn't look at me. "Not even a thank you."

"Why would you think he was going to thank you? He probably thinks we're the ones who doomed him."

He took a deep breath. "I know. And that sucks." He looked at me. "What other choice did we have? If we didn't say anything and The Families found him, he'd blame me. Now, he blames me for warning him. It was a situation we couldn't win."

I placed my hand on his thigh. "But at least we'll have a clear conscience. Whatever they do now, that's on them."

He took my hand in his. "You're right. I can't save them all. I knew that when I started this. It doesn't make it easier, but at least I know I'm doing the best I can." He forced a smile before putting the truck in gear. "What do you say we get a couple of hours of sleep before heading back to Dashton."

I patted his leg. "Sounds like a good plan to me."

He pulled out of the parking lot and headed for the jail.

I stared at him as we drove down the road. Quinn was always so confident, so sure of himself. Even in the most dire of situations, he remained calm. I had no doubts we'd be victorious in North Platte because Quinn was by my side. He had faith, so I did too. After the last few weeks, I could tell his confidence faltered, unraveling at the edges. He still tried to portray calmness and stay in control, but I could tell he didn't feel it. I doubted anyone else noticed, they didn't know him the same way I did. On one hand, it scared me that he was frightened. He was supposed to be the rock. On the other hand, it was refreshing. He was human. He didn't have to be strong all the time. He was allowed to have feelings. I knew no matter what lay ahead of us, we were going to face it together. We were going to be each other's support. We had to be. We couldn't count on anyone else.

CHAPTER 7

Quinn was really tired, and he slept soundly. I heard him snoring in the cell next to mine. Even after a cup of coffee, I was able to sleep for a few hours. It was nice. It helped refresh me. When I woke up, though, my shoulder ached. I wasn't quite ready to get up, so I lay in bed, hoping the pain would go away. I couldn't stop thinking about the conversation with Duncan, either. I realized the reason they had survived for so long was because they stayed out of other people's affairs. If I could live blissfully in a mall and bake cookies all day, I would do it too. But the outside world doesn't stay outside for long. It finds a way in. You can't ignore it. No matter how hard you try, eventually you have to face it. I wondered what they were going to do when they couldn't ignore it anymore. I wondered if they would try to find us, volunteer to help. I doubted it.

The pain grew so intense, I couldn't lay down anymore. I slowly sat up and draped my feet over the edge. I ran my hand down my face. I expected things to be difficult, especially since we dealt with and fought against people who were older and had more experience, but I never imagined it would be almost impossible. Looking back, we were lucky to overtake North Platte. The guards didn't have to give up as easily as they did. They could have fought bitterly. We would have eventually won. We had numbers on our side, but the death toll could have been a lot greater. We were also lucky when Mrs. Johnson's bodyguard came up. They could have wiped us out right then and there. Instead, they waited. It gave us enough time to get out and to safety. Well, relative safety. At least the workers had a better chance against zombies than they did against rocket launchers and helicopters.

As with everything, luck eventually runs out. Obviously, our supply was getting low. But that didn't mean we could give up. As much as I wanted to, as much as I wanted to tell Quinn I was done and wait for him at the ranch, I knew I couldn't. I knew my conscience would get the better of me. I couldn't live with that decision. I had to stick it out, see it to the end. Even if the end meant death. At least I would have tried. No one could fault me for that.

I stood from the bed and shuffled to the door. I untwisted the tie. I grunted and struggled against the metal, gritting my teeth. It wasn't easy doing it one handed, but I didn't want to wake Quinn. He needed to sleep. He needed to collect his thoughts. I finally got it undone and headed to the admissions desk. I opened the duffel bag and pulled out some painkillers and a bottle of water. I tilted my head back to swallow and stared at the ceiling. Taking a deep breath, I wondered what we were going to do next. The first priority was to take out Florida, but how were we going to do it? We were grossly outnumbered and out technologized. The one thing we did have was determination, and that won many wars. I hoped it was enough.

A slapping sound, like bare feet on linoleum, resounded through the room. I turned, expecting to see Quinn. No one was there. I walked to his cell and peered through the bars. He still lay on the bed, his back toward me. I shrugged and headed back to the desk. The sound came again, followed by a rustling. Confusion flowed through me as I looked around the room. Where was that sound coming from? The door was still shut, locked up tight. I knew the sound wasn't coming from my room. It had to be coming from Quinn's. What else could it be? I took another drink of my water. The slapping sounded again, a little louder, and I saw movement out of the corner of my eye. I turned to my left. I looked on the floor, at the corner of the admission's desk. The water flew out of my mouth. I wanted to scream, but the sound caught in my throat.

A zombie crawled across the floor. It was almost completely decomposed. The skin on her face was gray and flaking, the skull poking through in several areas. Her arms were bones, with the exception of the hand, which was still covered in a glove of skin. It hissed at me and increased its effort to pull itself forward. I took a step to the side and noticed it was missing a leg. I reached from my gun. Crap! I left my holster in my room. I turned to get it when a moan echoed through the room. I froze. Glancing over my shoulder and the desk, I noticed another creature climbing through the emergency hatch. He was in better shape than the other, but his skin was yellowed and his clothes almost completely ripped off. I could see his torso, a hole ripped through his chest. If his heart had been beating, I would have seen it.

"Quinn!" I screamed and headed to my cell. I grabbed my gun and went back into the main room.

I took out the man first. He wasn't the closest, but he was the bigger threat. He could move faster than the woman on the floor. The bang of the gun made my ears ring instantly after I fired the shot, but I couldn't worry about it. It was better to be deaf than consumed alive. The bullet hit the guy above the right temple. His head jerked back and he fell down the ladder. I turned my attention to the woman. She was a few steps in front of me, still hissing and grabbing for my legs. The bullet hit her in the top of the head. Brain, bone, and ichor sprayed into my face.

"Krista!" Quinn's voice called behind me.

I didn't have time to turn around. I ran to the trap door and looked down the hole. Several zombies were clambering over their fallen brother, trying to negotiate the ladder. I slammed the door shut. I grabbed the edge of the desk and tried to pull it over the door, but it was bolted to the floor. I felt hands on my arms and swung around.

"Krista, it's me." His voice sounded far off, like he was talking under water. "You okay?"

I took a deep breath and nodded, relaxing just a little. I turned to Quinn. His cheeks were puffed out as he let out a breath, his hands ran through his hair. Not the best way to be woken up.

"You scared the crap out of me," he said.

"You? Imagine how I felt seeing a zombie crawling through the trap door. How did they get up the ladder?"

He shook his head. "I don't know, but they did. We'd better get our stuff and get out of here."

I nodded my agreement and went to gather my things. As I turned, a pounding resounded on the stairwell door. Quinn and I stopped and looked. Was I hearing things? I had to be. My ears were still ringing from the gun shots. There was no way both of our exits were blocked by undead. We checked everything before going to sleep. The stairway was clear, and the door to the outside from the emergency exit was closed. They couldn't have gotten through both. They just couldn't. The pounding sounded louder. My heart fluttered, my breath came in gasps. I glanced at Quinn. His face was white.

"What are we gonna do?" I asked.

"We still have to get out of here. Get your stuff."

If it wasn't for the incredible pain in my shoulder, I would have thought I was in a dream. I shoved my stuff into my bag. It didn't take long, and within a few minutes, I was back in the main room with Quinn. He stood over the emergency exit, his hands on his hips, staring at the trap door.

"What? Is it clear?"

He shook his head. "No."

I bit my lip and stared from him to the stairwell door. The creatures still pounded mercilessly on the other side.

"How are we going to get out? We're trapped."

"We'll have to go up."

"Up? Like to the roof?"

He stared at me. He was annoyed. "What other choice do we have?"

I clenched my jaw, angry he would snap at me like that. I wanted to yell back at him, tell him this wasn't my fault and remind him we were in a jail, but I bit back the words. There was probably some other secret door hidden in the ceiling. There had to be another way in. Quinn knew what he was doing. I followed him down the hall with the cells. He placed his bags on the floor and glanced up. I followed his gaze. The ceiling was concrete blocks, like the rest of the walls in the area. My hope faltered. He jumped, trying to hit a block with his hands, but fell short.

"Grab me one of the chairs out there, would ya?"

I did as he asked, dragging the heavy metal chair across the floor. It made a god-awful scraping, which caused the pounding on the door to become more urgent, and I was sure I heard the trapdoor rattling. I hurried to the end of the hall. After giving Quinn the chair, I rushed back to the front of the hallway and closed the door. I felt a little safer with one more barrier between me and the undead.

Quinn climbed onto the seat and stretched up. He was still a little short, but he could reach the ceiling with his fingertips. He scraped the surface, and white chunks fluttered to the ground. Steadying himself on the wall with his left hand, he hopped from the chair and rammed his fist into the block. I was shocked when it went through. His fist was caught, and when he came back down, it tore a large chunk out of the block. I ran over to him and glanced up.

Darkness lay beyond. That didn't sit well with me. Logic dictated the chances of zombies being on the roof were slim to none, but who would have guessed they would be able to climb a ladder? I had visions of skeletons falling from the ceiling, burying us in snapping jaws. Quinn jumped and punched again. More stuff fell from the ceiling. I turned away to keep from getting it in my eyes. Something thudded behind me and hit my ankle. I jumped and turned, a small squeak escaping from my mouth. I still had my gun in my hand, and I was ready to use it. It was just the ceiling block, but I didn't relax. My hands were sweating, and I needed to pee. I looked back up. Quinn jumped again, trying to get a hold of something in the ceiling I couldn't see. It took him four tries, but he finally pulled down a knotted rope. He hopped down from the chair.

"I'm going to go up first. You hand me the bags, then I'll pull you up."

I nodded.

A knock resounded from the end of the hall. Both of our heads turned to the direction. I hurried down the hall and stopped at the door. Peering through the window, I scanned the admission room. I could see the corner of the trapdoor. It was open. They finally made it through. Another knock sounded, right next to the window. I glanced into the lifeless eyes of a zombie. Half of his face had rotted off. His mouth opened and closed on the glass, leaving a trail of yellow saliva. I double checked the lock on the door. It would hold. I turned back to Quinn. He was already up the rope. Laying on his stomach, his arms dangled out of the hole. I handed him the first bag. He tossed it into the darkness, followed by the second one.

"Step onto the bottom knot and hang on to another," he said.

I did as I was told, and he lifted me into the ceiling.

We dug our flashlights out of our bags and shone them around. The area was large enough for us to crouch in, our toes hung over the edge of the opening. Above us was another door. This one was metal. Quinn pushed on it, but it didn't budge.

"It's probably locked from the outside," he said.

He slammed his shoulder into it, and it moved slightly. He did it several more times, hoping to break the lock, but nothing happened.

"Shoot it."

He stared at me.

"Shoot the lock. It's the only way."

"You'll want to get back down. It's going to be loud."

I crouched down and covered my ears. "I'll be fine."

He fired two shots. Even though my ears were trying to recover from the earlier shots, I still thought my ear drums were going to explode. It was painful. I briefly wondered if my ears were bleeding, but I didn't have time to find out. The door popped open, and we clambered onto the roof.

The sun was low in the sky but still a few hours away from setting. I spun as I surveyed the area, my gun at the ready. There wasn't much on the roof, just some gravel and a couple of intakes. Once we realized everything was safe, Quinn slammed the door shut, then collapsed on top of it. I lowered my weapon. Out of the corner of my eye, something glinted in the distance. I turned to look at it. Two buildings away, the sunlight reflected off something. I squinted. From where I stood, it looked like a person looking through binoculars. He realized I was looking at him and disappeared.

"Did you see that?"

Quinn nodded. "Unfortunately, yes."

"What do you think it was?"

"Someone making sure we didn't get out of the building alive."

I jerked my head toward him, eyes wide. "What? You think those zombies were sent to attack us?"

Quinn took a deep breath and got to his feet. He brushed the white dust from the ceiling off his clothes, which didn't actually come off, but smeared it into the fabric.

"We checked everything last night. Nothing. We were secure. Yeah, the creatures could have gotten up the staircase, it's happened before. But there is no way they could have opened the door that leads outside from the trapdoor. It was locked from the inside. They're not smart enough to figure it out. I'm guessing someone alive opened it for them."

"But who?"

He stared at me, his head cocked to the side, the look on his face said I should know who did it.

"If I had to bet my life, I would say it was Duncan."

I let the information soak in for a moment. I guess if anyone wanted us out of the way, it would be him. He was the only one who knew we were in town, and he was the only one who knew where we were staying. We didn't tell him that was our plan, but apparently he had spies everywhere. Plus, we'd stayed there before. It was logical. But why would he want us dead? Why wouldn't he just let us go? He made it very clear he could get along without us, so why not live and let live?

"Why?" I was pretty sure I already knew the answer, but I wanted validation. I wanted to hear it out loud from someone else.

"He blames us." Quinn scanned the horizon. "I bet he thinks we're going to bring death to him and his friends." He turned his gaze back on me. "We're the only ones who know where he is. If we're dead, we can't show anyone else his hideout."

"So he's trying to protect those people."

He spit. "Yup."

I shook my head. "I guess he doesn't realize we're not trying to harm him. If we wanted to, why would we bother warning him about the helicopters?"

"People don't think logically in stressful situations. You know that. He's just trying to cover all his bases."

I reholstered my gun and placed my hand on my hip. "So now what? What do you think he'll do if he knows were still alive?"

Quinn sighed. "I don't know. But I think it's best we get out of here as soon as possible. He might not leave it up to the zombies to finish us off." He looked at me, his eyebrows raised. "And both of us know what kind of weapons he's carrying."

"Yeah. Let's head out."

We headed over to the side of the building and surveyed the scene. On the bright side, there was a ladder that led to the street. It wasn't going to be easy, but at least I could make it down with one hand. Zombies streamed in through the front door, and the alley where the truck was parked was full of undead. There was no way we were going to get to the truck unnoticed.

"What now?"

"We need a diversion. Something to draw them to the other side of the building."

"Like what? Live bait is out of the question. They'll spot you before you even make it to the ground, and we now know they can climb ladders. If they get up here, we're dead. We have nowhere else to go."

Quinn made his way to the other side of the building and glanced over the edge. It seemed so hopeless. If only I had the full use of my arm, it would make things a lot easier. Quinn took long strides back to me.

Death To The Undead

"There's another roof over there, about half way down the building." He pointed toward the edge. "I can shimmy down a pipe and make my way to the street. From there, I'll draw them away, and you can pick me up when you get the truck started."

I opened my mouth to protest, to tell him there was no way I could drive a stick shift with my arm in a sling, but I never got the chance. A boom tore through the sky. I felt a deep pressure on my chest, like someone was shoving me, and I was thrown onto my back. Everything went black. I came to a few seconds later. Every part of my body ached, my shoulder felt like it was in a vice. I opened my eyes and stared at the sky. A plume of black smoke blotted out the serene blue. I didn't have to look. I knew what happened. They blew up the semi. They really didn't want us to leave. I tried to push myself up on my elbow, but my body wouldn't comply. I lay back down and placed my hand on my forehead. Why was everyone trying to kill us?

CHAPTER 8

"The building is on fire!" Quinn pulled me up by my shoulders. He yelled, his face was red and his mouth was wide, but I barely heard him. "We have to get out of here!"

My body didn't want to cooperate. Every jerk and tug he gave me to get me to my feet were like needles being stabbed through my flesh. I was more than convinced my ears were permanently damaged. The ringing was replaced with soft static, like how you hear underwater. They even felt like they were flooded with the liquid. I touched one and examined my fingertip, convinced I would see blood. To my surprise, there wasn't any.

Quinn succeeded in getting me moving, and I followed him to the other side of the building. I was aware of the danger. I knew what would happen if we stayed on the roof. But I couldn't convince my muscles of the emergency. My feet were heavy. It felt like they were sticking to the roof, and I consciously had to will them to keep moving. I made it to the edge and collapsed, catching myself before careening over the side. There was another roof about half way down, but I was sure something would have broken in the fall. Quinn tossed our bags over the side. A puff of dust rose. I waited for the whump, but didn't hear anything. I was just thankful there wasn't anything fragile in there, though I doubted all of the bottled waters made it out unscathed.

Death To The Undead

I looked at Quinn. He fastened a nylon rope around his waist. It was one we always kept in our bag for emergencies, but I didn't think it was thick enough to actually do any good. It could have tied our bags up into a tree if need be, but other than that, it seemed almost worthless. I knew what he planned. There was no way I could shimmy down a pipe to the roof. My arm wouldn't allow it. I just didn't think the plan would work. He approached and laced the rope around my waist.

"I'm going to lower you down," he said.

Well, it was pretty close to what he said. I couldn't really hear him.

"Are you sure the rope will hold?"

He shrugged. "I hope so. If not, it's not that far of a fall."

I glanced over the edge again. It may not have been deadly if I fell, but I still didn't want to experience it. I had enough pain to deal with, I didn't want to add more. I crossed my mental fingers, hoping the rope would hold.

"You ready?"

I sat on the edge and swung my legs over. "No, but do I have another choice?"

He took up the slack in the rope and I slid my butt of the building. There was a small jerk as I was suspended in the air as he caught my weight. He slowly let the slack out, and I bobbed toward the second roof. I kept an eye on him and the landing and made sure I didn't bounce off the side of the building. My jaw was sore from clenching it, adding to the pain that already flowed through my body. An eternity later, my feet touched the solid surface. I waved with my good hand to let him know I was down. He nodded, then grabbed the drainpipe and slid down.

I glanced over the side toward the street. A few zombies milled around, but they weren't paying attention to us. If anything, they'd be drawn to the explosion. At least I hoped so. We still weren't sure how they tracked people. In any case, we'd be able to make it down, then we'd have to run like mad. God, I hoped my body would allow me to do that. Quinn stood next to me and took up the slack in the rope.

"Where are we going once we're down?" I asked.

"Back to the mall."

I might not have been able to hear very well, but I couldn't mistake the anger in his voice. I assumed he wanted to find Duncan and put him through the same death he attempted to put us through. I know that's what I wanted to do. I wanted him to suffer, hear him scream, and see him eaten bit by bit. How dare he put us through this when all we wanted to do was make sure he was safe. He deserved a horrific death, and I wanted to be the one who gave it to him. It wasn't the nicest thought, I know. My hatred for Duncan at that moment rivaled my loathing for Liet. Forget compassion. It's hard to care about how the history books were going to tell your story when you have to shimmy down a building to save your life.

Death To The Undead

Quinn signaled he was ready, so I went over the side. This trip down was a lot faster than the first. I assumed it was because there were zombies in the neighborhood and he didn't want me to be a piñata. When my feet touched the concrete, I pulled out my gun and stood ready. I shot a couple of creatures in the area. I'm not sure if they noticed me, but I wasn't going to take the chance. It only took one moan. The bags plopped onto the ground next to me. One of them almost hit me, but that was my fault, I walked in circles, trying to take in my entire surroundings. Still, I looked up at Quinn with a scowl. He cringed and mouthed "Sorry" before heading down the drain pipe.

Once he was on the ground, I went for one of the bags. He stopped me.

"We'll come back for those," he said. "We need to find a vehicle."

I glanced around the street. There were plenty of abandoned cars sitting around, but they'd been sitting there for years. More than likely, the batteries were dead or they didn't have keys or they were occupied by undead. The situation sucked. There was no other way to put it. We ran through zombie-filled streets with nothing but our wits and what ammunition we had left. There was the distinct possibility we would die or get bitten. The one thing that kept me moving was my intense anger. I was so mad at Duncan and his people, I would have jumped through fire to make sure I got my revenge.

The adrenaline pumped through my veins, making it a easier to move. I still couldn't hear very well, but my sense of sight and smell heightened. At least it felt like it did. Quinn and I stayed close to each other, shoulder to shoulder, and made our way methodically down the street. It wasn't any different than clearing a building. We stayed alert and in contact so we didn't accidentally shoot one another. We checked the first vehicle that looked like it might run. It was a compact car. It was small and not my first choice, but anything was better than being on foot. I would have taken a go-cart at that moment.

Quinn stood guard while I checked the door. Locked. I glanced in the window. If there were keys, it might be worth breaking the window to get in. Nothing. I turned to Quinn and jerked my head to the side. We continued down the street.

The next car we came to was an SUV, which would have worked out great. It had plenty of room and was well protected. I went up to the window and glanced in. Keys were inside. I reached for the handle. Something slammed against the back window. I jumped back. A young girl, probably no more than 12, smashed against the glass. Her black hair was stringy, her face gray with black spots where the flesh was about to fall off. Her teeth clicked against the window as she snapped at me. I took a deep breath, and we moved on.

My hope faltered, and the streets were getting more crowded with the walking dead. Luckily, none of the creatures had spotted us, but that could change at any moment. I was surprised we hadn't been seen. Why didn't they notice us? We weren't hiding; we were walking down the middle of the street. Quinn even killed a few creatures who came too close. But none of them moaned, not one of them sounded the dinner bell.

We came to an extended cab truck. I didn't hold out any hope. After the last two, I was sure we'd be running the entire way back to Dashton. I glanced in. The keys were in the ignition. That was lucky. I pulled on the handle and opened the door. Finally! Something went our way. I turned the key. The engine turned over but didn't start. I tried again. Same thing. Quinn stood with his back against the truck.

"Anything?" he whispered.

I poked my head out, annoyed he would even ask. Couldn't he hear? "Nothing." I tried to keep my anger in check. I wasn't mad at him. He was in the same situation I was. Yelling wouldn't help anything.

"Our chances of finding something on the street are not good," I told him. "We have to find something that wasn't abandoned. Like a car dealership or something."

He wiped the sweat from his forehead with the back of his hand. "The closest place is five blocks away." He pointed to the right.

"We've made it this far. We have to chance it."

I climbed out of the truck and took one step when it happened. The moment I'd been dreading since we got off the roof. A low, loud moan echoed through the streets. I glanced at Quinn, his face was a reflection of mine: disbelief and anger. Zombies crawled out of everywhere, from under cars, from buildings, from cars that were open, and converged on our position. There was no way we were going to make it to the end of the block, let alone five to find a car.

I jumped back into the truck cab. Quinn fired at the closest of the creatures. The truck whirred again. I pumped the gas. I knew it wasn't going to start. I didn't know a lot about cars, but I knew the whir, whir, whir wasn't a good sound. Tears threatened to fall as my life flashed before my eyes. That street was going to be my grave. I turned the key again. Whir, whir, whir. I slammed the steering wheel and pumped the gas a few more times.

"C'mon!" I screamed.

I turned the key again. The engine roared to life. I stared at the wheel, confused, not believing I heard what I actually heard. For a moment, I thought it was all in my imagination. Then, I thought maybe I was dead. Maybe a zombie grabbed me from under the vehicle and devoured me on the street, but in my mind, I was still in the truck.

The passenger door slammed shut, and I turned to look. Quinn was next to me, sweat on his forehead, horror on his face. Beyond him, through the window, the zombies closed in. A few more steps and they'd be at the truck. Still, I was convinced the truck wasn't really running.

Death To The Undead

"What are you waiting for?" Quinn asked. "Go, go, go!"

I put the truck in gear, slamming my foot onto the gas. The tires squealed before pushing the truck down the road.

The zombie horde was huge. I couldn't move the truck anywhere without hitting an undead. The truck bounced and bucked its way through the streets, blood and body parts covered every inch of the outside. Keeping control bordered on impossible. I only had one hand and attempted to drive at a high rate of speed. The truck wasn't as protected as a semi. It was way lower to the ground, making it possible for the creatures to break the windows. Plus, it was a lot lighter, so if enough of them surrounded us, they could tip us over. I had to get out of the crowd as quickly as possible.

Something clunked in the bed of the truck. I glanced in the rearview, but couldn't see anything. Quinn heard it too, he turned in his seat, gun in hand, waiting. The creature plastered itself against the back window, pounding on the glass. I jerked the wheel to the right. The zombie flew to one side but didn't fall out. It tried to regain its balance, but I zigzagged through the streets. A group of five creatures emerged in front of me, and I pressed further on the gas. Two of them bounced off the side, one went over the top, and the other two were sucked under the tires. I'm pretty sure we caught air, and we came down hard. The creature in the back bounced out. I glanced in my side view and saw his head shatter in blood and bone on the sidewalk. After a few blocks, the zombies thinned, the road cleared, and I was able to ease up on my speed. As a moving target, they still followed after us, but we could outrun them. I headed toward the mall.

I pulled into the parking lot and put the truck into park. There was no way to sneak up on the mall, no secret entrance we could take so Duncan and his people couldn't see us coming. Even if there was, I probably wouldn't have taken it. I was infuriated. I wanted them to see me coming. I wanted them to know vengeance was on its way. I half expected to have been gunned down before making it that far, but was thankful we weren't. We stared at the building. The particleboards that usually covered the windows had been torn off. A few articles of clothing and a suitcase lay in front of the doors. A zombie lurched around the corner and walked freely into the store. Quinn sighed next to me.

"They left."

"What?" I jerked my head to the side to stare at him. "Where would they go?"

Quinn shook his head. "Who knows? I'm sure they have another safe house somewhere. That guy we saw on the roof was probably the last to leave. I bet they left five minutes after we did."

I wanted to hunt them down, find out where they had gone. It wasn't fair. They couldn't just up and leave after sentencing us to death. I felt cheated. I wanted my revenge. In actuality, though, I wouldn't have gone through with actually feeding Duncan to the zombies. Liet shot me, and he was still alive. I was pretty confident I would have punched Duncan, however. I couldn't let him get away without some punishment.

I looked at Quinn. "Do you want to go in? Just to make sure?"

He shook his head. Disappointment covered his face. He probably had visions of revenge dancing through his mind, pushing him through the zombie-infested streets, and they were dashed, just like mine.

"Nah. We need to get back. Figure out what that building is behind the caves and formulate a plan for invading Florida."

"Do you want to head back and get our stuff?"

He thought for a moment. "No. I think we'll just leave it there for a while. Even with the creatures following us, there were still so many. I doubt the place is safe. It's just some clothes and food. We'll get it later."

I nodded. "Okay. Works for me." I rubbed my shoulder. "Do you think you can drive?"

"Oh, yeah, sure." He tossed his guns in the backseat and opened his door.

I scooted over to the passenger seat and leaned my head against the headrest.

Quinn put the truck in gear, and we headed to the highway.

"Do you think the spotter saw us?" I asked as we drove out of town.

"At the mall?"

I nodded.

Quinn sighed. "I don't know. It's hard to say. If he was smart, he would have just high-tailed it out of there after the truck exploded."

"Do you think they'll come after us?"

Quinn glanced at me. "No. They wouldn't waste their time."

"How can you be so sure?"

"Because we don't know where they went. If we followed them and threatened their new sanctuary, I'm sure they would just shoot us on the spot. They'll fade back into the shadows and live their lives like this never happened. I doubt we'll ever see them again."

I placed my foot on the dashboard. "For their sake, I hope we don't."

Quinn placed both hands on the wheel. His knuckles turned white as he gripped it tighter.

"Yeah, I have to agree with you. That was pretty messed up what they did. But you can't blame them."

I chuckled. "Oh, yes I can. And I will. The last thing we need is another bounty for our heads. There's already enough people trying to kill us."

We both sat in silence for a while. I replayed the whole scene from the jail in my head. We were lucky to get out alive, especially with the shape I was in. My hearing started to come back, along with the ringing in my ears. I hoped that wouldn't last for too long. My whole body hurt, too. Every muscle felt like it was on fire, and my bones ached. My shoulder hurt so bad it pulsed. I desperately wished I had a pain killer, but those were in the bags lying in the street. It made me hate Duncan and his crew that much more. It made me continue to hate Liet, too. I wanted so badly to make him feel like I did, to shoot him in the shoulder and see how well he handled it. If he was still in our possession, I probably would do it. It would relieve a lot of anger and make me feel better. Too bad he wasn't still in our possession.

"Do you think they found Liet?" I asked.

Quinn clicked his tongue. "I doubt it. He's not stupid. He won't go back to the camp. He'll head to Florida. He's needs backup if he wants to take us down."

I looked out the window. That was the first thought to cross my mind, too, but I was never sure with Liet. He didn't always act logically. I chewed on my thumbnail. I really hoped he headed to Florida, but something at the back of my brain told me not to count on it. I hoped I was being overly cautious.

CHAPTER 9

In the time we were gone, the survivors placed a barricade across the only road into Dashton. It was a tree, so it looked like it happened naturally. It wouldn't raise suspicion. They also had lookouts in the forest on either side. If someone did try and get into our safe haven uninvited, they wouldn't make it far.

Quinn pulled up to the log and slowed, cursing under his breath. At that point, we didn't realize it was done on purpose. He leaned forward and glanced out the windshield, sizing up how easy it would be to move the tree. The bushes on my side of the truck rustled, and a worker stepped up to the road, an automatic weapon slung across his chest. He glanced into the truck and signaled the others. I rolled down the window.

"Sorry, guys. We didn't realize it was you. Didn't you take a semi out?"

I scowled. "Yes. We ran into some trouble."

"Sorry to hear that. You'll be back at camp in no time." He turned and disappeared into the trees.

The others moved the tree out of the way, swinging it open like a gate. I glanced out the back window and wondered how they rigged it to do that. It was a short-lived curiosity. I was just happy they looked out for everyone's well being.

We parked the truck next to the other vehicles and stepped out. My knees gave out and I almost fell, but I caught myself on the door handle. I still couldn't believe how sore I was. It bordered on ridiculous. My first task was to find some pain pills and something to eat. I took a few cautious steps on shaky legs. When I knew they weren't going to give out, I went to find a First Aid kit.

Quinn and I met at the fire after I found what I looked for. The group had made a stew, and we ate heartily. They wanted to know what happened out there. The looks of defeat on our faces increased curiosity, along with the fact we lost a semi. Nobody asked, though, and we weren't ready to talk about it. There was no point in causing any more undue stress. The survivors had enough to worry about, they didn't need to know more humans might try to kill them. Besides, the events were too fresh, too real. The emotions ran deep, and I doubted either Quinn or I could get through the story without getting overly agitated. Eventually, we'd tell the story. When it didn't irritate every fiber of our being. Pam sat across from us at the fire, and she would surely ask what happened. Of course I would tell her, and then it wouldn't take long for the story to get out. That was a nice thing about such a small community, but it was also the bad thing. One person could twist the facts and panic would follow. I hoped it didn't happen, but I wouldn't be surprised if it did.

The pill took effect. My body was still sore, but the pain didn't border on unbearable. Quinn put his arm around my shoulder, and I snuggled closer to him. We stared at the fire. In any other circumstance, it would have been romantic. It was still pleasant, but far from ideal. One day, I told myself. One day we'll be able to spend every night like this and not have to worry about anything. However, given the recent happenings, I highly doubted that day would ever come.

"So, do I actually have to ask, or are you just going to tell me?" Pam held her hands out to her sides, an anxious look on her face.

Quinn sighed. "They tried to kill us."

"Who?"

"The survivors in Casper. They sent zombies to attack us while we were sleeping in the jail."

"Why?" Pam's forehead wrinkled in confusion. She placed her hands in her lap and leaned forward.

I sat up reluctantly. "Who knows? I can only speculate that it was because they thought we would endanger them since we knew where they were hiding. I'm sure they thought by getting rid of us, they could ensure their safety. We tried to go back and confront them, but they were gone when we got there."

Pam stared at us for a minute. "Are you sure?"

I threw my hand into the air and slapped it back on my leg. "Well, no. But we couldn't exactly find them to ask them. They fled from the mall."

Pam averted her gaze to the ground and picked at some pine needles. She threw them into the fire. "Seems like a lot of hassle to go through. They could have just disappeared and you'd never know where they went. Why did they need to kill you?"

"Who knows?" Quinn said quietly. "All I know is that we don't have to worry about them anymore. If they want to take care of themselves, then they can. I'm done babysitting others."

Tanya made her way to the fire and took a seat to my right. I stared at her for a moment, then focused my gaze back on Pam.

"Any news about Liet?"

"Nah. He's long gone. We haven't seen any trace of him. But to be sure, we've placed guards in strategic places around the camp. He won't get back in without someone knowing. In fact, no one will get in without someone knowing."

"Have you had any trouble from the tunnel?" Quinn's voice was laced with implication.

"Nope. Nothing."

"Has anyone been out there to explore what's out there?"

Pam shook her head. "No. We figured we'd wait until you got back. We didn't want to worry anyone needlessly."

Quinn nodded. "Good plan. We'll take care of that first thing tomorrow." He stretched his arms above his head and yawned. "I'm beat. I'm going to bed." He leaned forward and kissed me softly on the lips before heading into the cave.

I watched him leave, then leaned back on my elbow and stared at the flames.

"Sounds like you had quite the adventure in Casper," Pam commented.

I snorted. "It's not the kind of fun I normally like to have."

"Well, if anyone was going to come out of it alive, it was you two. You're too crafty to go down."

Normally, I would have smiled at the comment. It was good to know I wasn't just lucky, but that I had some skill too and others recognized it. It was especially nice coming from Pam. She was the one who trained me. But with the amount of pain still radiating through my body, I couldn't find the desire to be thankful. We were lucky, there was no denying it. We survived a horde attack and an explosion. In reality, though, it wasn't that hard. The zombies were slow, stupid, it didn't take much to get away from them. They had numbers on their side, that was their only advantage. If they cornered you, you were done for. But you had to be smart enough not to get cornered. Every once in a while, they would surprise an unsuspecting victim, pop out of a hiding place. I never understood how that happened. Was the victim not paying attention? Zombies are predictable. They are simple. So how did they destroy the world?

"Must have been scary out there, surrounded by all those zombies." Tanya spoke quietly, her eyes glued to her lap.

I readjusted so I could face her. "It had its moments, yeah. But Quinn was with me, I knew I'd be all right."

She lifted her head and stared at me. "Must be nice knowing someone's got your back."

I was a little shocked at the comment and didn't really know how to respond. I glanced at Pam, who shrugged, then back to Tanya. I was still trying to get used to her presence. The last time I talked to her in Florida, she was gung-ho about helping the rebellion. She couldn't wait to be a part of history and topple the evil tyrannical regime. At that moment, she seemed to struggle just living. She had no motivation.

Granted, she did lose her father and thought it was our fault. She became hell-bent on getting revenge, but when she found out we didn't do it, what was she going to do? What defined her life and gave her meaning was suddenly gone. It didn't help that Quinn was mad at her. She did allow his best friends to get arrested by The Families. She was lost. She wanted to belong, but she didn't know how.

"It is." I didn't know what else to say. "Everyone here has yours, you know. No one is going to let anything bad happen to you."

Her face crumpled and she burst into tears. She buried her face in her hands and sobbed quietly. Wide eyed, I looked at Pam.

"What's going on?" I mouthed.

Pam shook her head.

"I told them!" Tanya blurted. "I told them everything!"

The anger instantly flushed my cheeks, and I set my jaw. My stomach fluttered, my throat tightened. I wanted to give her the benefit of the doubt, believe she was talking about something else, but I knew what she meant. I knew what she'd done. I wanted to jump on top of her and beat her bloody, but I refrained. It wasn't easy, but I stayed in control. I sat silently, waiting for her to finish. She slowly lifted her head from her hands and wiped her eyes on her sleeves.

That actually explained quite a lot. I always wondered how she got from Florida to Nebraska in Bill and Kyle's car by herself. She didn't have any weapons. Where did she stop for gas? I didn't have time to dwell on it, though, we had more pressing matters to tend to. After her confession, I knew she didn't have to worry about it. She drove from one military outpost to the next until she found us.

"I know you hate me. I know you're mad at me, but I didn't know what else to do. And if it makes you feel better, it took me a couple hours before I said anything."

Oh, yeah, that made me feel tons better.

"Why don't you tell us what happened?"

Thank goodness Pam was there. She read my mind. I was afraid if I opened my mouth, I would lose it and yell at Tanya. That wouldn't get us anywhere.

"It was right after the incident with my dad. I went back to the coffee house, in shock."

She crossed the street in my mind, making her way to a table and sitting down heavily. She stared at the table top, her hands folded in her lap, wondering if what happened actually happened. She told herself it was a dream. All a dream. Bill came downstairs to get a drink and noticed her. He asked if she was all right, but she didn't hear him. He touched her arm, jerking her back into reality.

"You all right? You look pale?"

"I...I'm fine," Tanya squeaked out. She wanted to say something, tell him what happened, but she couldn't find the words. She felt if she said it out loud, it would make it real, and she still wasn't sure if it was.

"Well, if you need anything, you just let me know. Kyle and I are going to have to head back soon, though. We can't stay here forever."

Tanya nodded mechanically, focusing her gaze back on the tabletop.

That night, while they settled down for the evening, Tanya turned on the TV, hoping to get her mind off the events of the day. An emergency news bulletin took over all the channels. The story was about the semi that returned from North Platte, the semi with the zombies in it.

"It's outrageous!" The newscaster was on the brink of yelling. "They are jealous of our existence. They want to wipe us out." He placed his elbow on his desk and leaned forward, his right hand pointing at the screen. "They tell you they want to make the world safe, they want us to be able to leave Florida, but they can't guarantee your safety. They have no control over the zombies, and they have no way to kill them. This wall, this drain on our resources, was supposed to keep the creatures at bay, but it won't and hasn't worked. The people in North Platte are probably already dead. The only safe place left is Florida. Think of your children. Think of your neighbor. Do you really want to go out there?

"We take you now to the recorded carnage of what happened earlier today. A convoy returned from North Platte with a truck full of supplies, to find that clothing and food were not the only things stored in the back."

The scene cut away to the back of the truck and the workers unloading the supplies. They carted the stuff away on dollies when a muffled scream rose from the trailer. They ran to the back to see what happened. Within seconds, they moved away from the truck, more screams filled the air, accompanied by moaning. A girl ran to the truck, ready to jump in, but she was stopped. The camera switched angles, and Tanya's shocked face filled the screen.

Bill and Kyle focused on her. Tanya's tears rolled down her face. She tried to convince herself it hadn't happened, but watching it on TV made it impossible to deny. She wanted to scream, to throw things, to punch a wall, but she couldn't get off the couch.

"The people in North Platte didn't do that," Kyle's voice broke through her sadness.

She looked at him, but she didn't really see him.

"They would never do something like that."

She sucked in a deep breath, and the tears stopped flowing. Her sadness was replaced by a near uncontrollable rage. She clenched her jaw and balled her fists. How did they know if North Platte sent the zombies or not? They'd been down in Florida.

"You don't know." Her voice came out in a whisper.

"Yes, I do," Kyle said. "They would never do something like that."

Tanya got up and left the room. She wanted to shout, to tell him they did do it. They knew they couldn't win, they knew they were outnumbered, so they sent their backup plan. The original plan was to attack at the same time. They knew it was impossible, so they took over North Platte and decided to even the odds. If the majority of Florida were zombies, they would be easier to take down.

She paced back and forth in her bedroom. It made sense. Florida was the only safe place, and they were trying to take it away. It wasn't fair. Just because they wanted to live in zombie-infested lands, that didn't mean everyone did. And why did they have to kill her dad? What had he ever done to any of them? She was going to get even. She was going to make them pay.

She headed out the front door. Bill or Kyle called after her, but she had a mission. She made her way to the Johnson High School.

"Hi," the girl behind the front desk said. "How can I help you today?"

"I need to see Mrs. Johnson immediately."

The girl's eyes grew wide. "Hey, aren't you the girl from the news?"

Tanya didn't answer.

The girl picked up the phone, and Tanya was on the elevator a few minutes later.

"They said they weren't going to hurt them." Tanya moved closer to me, her hand outstretched, close to my knee.

I felt repulsed by her presence. I wanted to slap her hand away, but I knew if I moved, I would do more than slap.

"They said they were just going to ask them a few questions. Then, they told me if I wanted to make it up to them, I had to do something."

She was close, within inches. I couldn't look at her face. I was focused on her hand. I knew if she touched me, I would burst into flames or get some horrific disease. I tried to move away without her noticing.

"They told me if I came here and captured you, I would be forgiven for stashing the guns."

Pam's laugh was loud. I looked at her. What could she possibly find so funny? Tanya betrayed us. She turned in Bill and Kyle, and she was going to take me back to Florida, probably to my execution, all because she lost her father and her mind.

Pam collected herself. "And you believed them?"

Tanya looked hurt, like Pam just told her that her favorite pet had been run over.

"At the time, yes."

"Wow." Pam stifled a few more chuckles. "You do realize they were hoping you'd die, right? It was all part of their plan from the beginning."

Tanya sniffed and pulled her hand back. "I realize that now. I was so stupid." She punched her forehead. "Stupid, stupid, stupid!"

Part of me knew I should probably stop her from hurting herself, but the other part wanted me to let her do it. She needed some punishment, why not let her give it to herself?

"Well, you can't change it now." My voice was low, menacing. I didn't mean for it to sound so evil, but what she did was unforgivable. It was rotten. She sentenced two of our best soldiers to death. Quinn was going to be pissed.

She stopped hitting herself and stared at me. "I know. But I want to make it up to you."

"How?"

"I want to help you invade Florida."

I scowled. "And how are we going to do that? We have no weapons. No way to fight them."

"I have an idea." Her face lit up as she spoke.

There was something in her eyes that didn't make me comfortable. A glint or spark of treachery. How could I trust her after what she did? Maybe she was truthful about wanting to help, but she was going to have to prove it to me.

"You know," I snarled, "I think I've heard enough from you for one night. We can handle the planning of Florida." I stood from the fire. "Pam, keep an eye on her."

Tanya huffed. "I'm not going anywhere. C'mon, hear me out."

I stared down at her. "Maybe tomorrow. And don't say anything about what you just told me to Quinn." I pointed my finger at both of them. "He will kill you." I turned and stomped into the cave.

I found a place to lay down and stared at the ceiling. I still didn't understand why everyone wanted to kill me. How did I go from being a nobody to being the country's most wanted? Granted, there weren't a lot of people left, but they all seemed to be gunning for me. I rolled onto my side and placed my hand under my head. How was I going to get myself out of this mess?

Death To The Undead

CHAPTER 10

The throb of pain woke me. I didn't know how long I'd been asleep, but I knew it wasn't long enough. My eyes were dry and gritty, my head fuzzy with the half-awake half-asleep feeling. I rolled onto my back and stared at the ceiling.

What were we going to do with Tanya? She'd betrayed us, jeopardized everything we'd worked for, and turned in Quinn's friends. Probably even sentenced them to death. She couldn't be trusted. It was as simple as that. I had such high hopes she had changed, that she wasn't the same girl I knew in high school, but she hadn't. She was still self-centered and looking out for number one.

Quinn was going to be so mad. How many times had he told me we had to attack North Platte and Florida at the same time? We didn't have the numbers, so we needed to rely on surprise. I talked him out of it. I convinced him the people in North Platte didn't have time that Liet was going to destroy them. Eventually, he would have, but he also needed them. The wall wouldn't get built. He knew how far to push them.

In reality, the reason I pushed Quinn so hard was for my own selfish reason. I hated Liet. I wanted him to pay. I wanted revenge for the way he treated me. I didn't consider the big picture, how my actions would affect others. I wanted results, and I wanted them quickly. I wasn't much different than Tanya, so it was unfair for me to be mad at her. She acted on impulse, like I did. The only person who had any right to be angry was Quinn.

How was he going to react when he found out what Tanya did? He was pretty good at keeping his emotions in check, keeping his anger under control. Where did he learn that? Did his dad teach him how to remain calm in adverse situations? What would my dad have said? Or my mom?

No doubt they would have been disappointed. They would have never actually said they were disappointed, but they would have given me the look. Their faces would have been pinched with a combination of anger and sadness. Dad's hands would be on his hips, and he would shrug and say, "Well, you're old enough to make your own decisions, you're old enough to deal with the consequences."

Mom wouldn't have said anything. She would have shaken her head and continued to do whatever she was doing. Then, at night when she tucked me in, she would have talked about emotion and their power over our actions.

"Sometimes," she would say, "we get so angry, the only way we think we are going to feel better is by making the person who made us angry feel as bad as we do. We do something mean and hurtful. We don't stop and think about the consequences those actions will have in the future, we just act. Sometimes, the best thing to do when someone makes you angry is nothing at all. The universe has a way of making people pay for their actions, and you'll have to pay for the bad things you do, too."

Death To The Undead

I remembered the lecture well. She gave it to me after Carmen made fun of me in the lunchroom and I dumped my tray of food on her. I'm sure they would have repeated it if they knew about Liet and the rebellion.

What did they know? They didn't hear the other kids laughing at me. They weren't the ones chained to the bed. The universe may even the score eventually, but I needed my vengeance sooner. But then again, maybe they had known something. It was a shame it was too late to know.

Quinn seemed to handle things much better than I did. He didn't seem driven by his emotions. He wasn't uncaring, he was just more logical. Still, he was human, and every person had a breaking point. With all that had happened with Bill and Kyle, I was sure Quinn was getting close to the edge.

My shoulder throbbed more, so I decided to get up and find some pain killers. I opted not to go for the heavy-duty ones but for regular ibuprofen. We were going to explore the backside of the mountain, and I needed my senses sharp.

I stepped out of the cave into the gray, cool morning. It was as I expected, I hadn't slept nearly long enough. The fires from the night before were still being tended. The group set up a 24-hour watch, just in case Liet came back or the helicopters made it that far up the mountain. I figured either case was unlikely, but it was better to be cautious.

Pam was at one of the rings, setting a coffee pot in the coals. She nodded as I approached.

"How'd you sleep?"

I massaged my sore shoulder and pulled my head to one side, an attempt to stretch the muscles. "Not good. I don't think my shoulder is ever going to stop hurting."

"Oh, sure it will. You've got to give it time." She signaled for me to come closer. "Let's have a look at it."

I sat next to her and slid the sling strap over my head. My arm felt weak and exposed, as if I removed its only protective layer. Sharp pains zipped through my back as I attempted to remove my shirt. Pam helped, but it was still excruciating. She ran her fingers over my skin. It felt like static electricity. Sparks of pain shot across my shoulder. Instinctively, I moved away.

"You've still got some swelling back here. I would tell you the best course of action is to stay at camp and rest, but I'm sure I would just be wasting my breath."

I attempted to pull my shirt back on. "Yes, you would. You know I can't just sit around."

Pam clicked her tongue. "Well, at least put an ice pack on it while you eat breakfast. I'll get you one." She stood.

"Hey, Pam," I called after her. She turned to look at me. "Where's Tanya? I thought I told you to keep an eye on her?"

"Why? What's wrong with Tanya?" A voice asked behind me.

I didn't have to turn to know it was Quinn. Dang it! That was the last thing I wanted him to hear. I scrambled for an excuse.

"She's just been having a hard time adjusting," Pam spoke. "Krista wanted me to make sure she's all right."

I mouthed a thank you to her. Quinn sat down next to me.

"Oh. I'm sure she'll be fine." He picked up a stick and stirred the fire.

"I'll go grab an ice pack." Pam pointed over her shoulder, then left.

"How are you doing this morning?" Concern laced his voice.

I winced. "I'm all right. I just wish my stupid shoulder would heal."

He wrapped his arm around me and pulled me close to him. I snuggled into his chest.

"It'll heal in time. You know, Pam was right. You really should stay here and rest."

I pushed myself up so I looked into his eyes. "I'm not staying in camp."

Quinn chuckled. "I am well aware of that. But if you won't rest, then you can't complain about the pain." He raised his eyebrows.

I rolled my eyes and settled back against his body. "Fine. I won't complain about the pain."

Pam returned with the ice pack and an Ace bandage and strapped the pack to my shoulder. It was uncomfortable, but the coldness did take away some of the pain. Quinn opened a can of salmon and heated it over the fire. The salty aroma of fish filled the air, and my stomach growled. When it was heated through, he handed me a plate filled with pink meat and crackers. I greedily scooped the food into my mouth.

Tanya showed up when I was half way through my breakfast. I stared at her as she sat across from me, my eyes narrowed. I hoped my brain waves penetrated her mind and she would remember our conversation from the night before. The last thing I needed was for her to say something to Quinn. He handed her a plate without saying a word. She picked at it delicately, her eyes flicking from me to Quinn. I knew she wanted to say something. I really hoped she didn't.

We finished eating, and Pam removed the ice pack from my back and helped me back into my sling. My arm felt better, the pain subsided. I knew it wasn't going to last, though. I knew once I stood up and walked through the cave, the irritation would return. Maybe Pam and Quinn were right. Maybe I should stay in camp. I was tired, and I needed a nap. But I knew I wouldn't sleep. I knew I would lay awake, wondering what Quinn was doing, hoping he was safe. The pain was intolerable, yeah, but it wasn't as overbearing as worrying about Quinn. I had to go with him. I had to know he was safe. I couldn't stand to lose him. He was all I had left.

Quinn stood and stretched. "I guess we'd better head out. I want to take care of this in the daylight."

I nodded and grabbed his hand, pulling myself to my feet. "Good idea. Pam, Tanya, you ready?"

Quinn glanced sideways at me. "I think we can handle this."

"Probably. But it's always nice to have some backup."

He turned so his back was to Tanya and he was close to my ear. "I don't think it's a very good idea if she goes with us. She has no zombie-killing skills."

Quinn was right. She didn't have any experience killing the undead, but I wasn't comfortable leaving her in camp. What if she ran away? What if she had a way to contact Florida? If she was with me, I knew she couldn't do anything nefarious. I could've left her with Pam, but she didn't seem to think keeping an eye on Tanya was top priority. I needed her by my side. I needed to know she wasn't going to betray us again.

"This will be a good opportunity to teach her some," I whispered. "With any luck, there won't be any creatures, and she'll learn how to sweep an area. Worst-case scenario, there are a few creatures and she learns how to shoot them."

Quinn placed his hands on his hips and glanced over his shoulder at her, letting a slow breath out of his nose. He turned back to me.

"Fine. But I'm not going to be responsible for her. If anything happens, that's on you."

I nodded. "I can live with that."

"Where's her gun?"

Crap! I didn't think of her needing a gun. If I had it my way, she wouldn't have any weapon, but then Quinn would be suspicious, and I'd have to tell him about what she did.

It's not that I didn't think Quinn should know, it was just that I didn't know what he'd do. It was obvious he was upset his friends were prisoners in Florida. If he knew it was all Tanya's fault, would he completely lose his mind? I needed him to be strong, to stay focused on what we had to do, I didn't want to risk him leaving and heading back to the ranch. We still had a lot to do, and a lot of people counting on us. I needed his help.

"I have a gun Krista gave me when we left North Platte," Tanya spoke quietly. "I think I left it on my bed. I can grab it before we go into the tunnel."

Quinn nodded. "Okay, then. Let's head out."

He headed toward the cave. Pam followed right behind him, staring at me with eyebrows raised, questioning what I was doing. I waved my hand, dismissing her concerns. She looked up at me.

"If any thought of harming us crosses your mind," I pointed a finger at her, "be rest assured that I am faster and I will not hesitate."

She paled slightly. "I'm not going to do anything. I told you, I want to make it up to you."

I gestured with an open hand toward the cave. "After you."

She turned and stepped into the darkness. We went to her sleeping bag and she grabbed her weapon. She fashioned the belt around her waist and adjusted the gun so it sat comfortably. We caught up to Pam and Quinn.

Death To The Undead

The tunnels felt tighter, the air thinner. I was sure it was because I was nervous, wondering what Tanya was going to do. I wanted to believe I was being overly cautious, I really did. I mean, Tanya seemed to be genuine. She sounded like she truly wanted to help us, but I'd fallen for that before. I couldn't ignore the fact that Pam left her alone, even after I told her not to, and Tanya didn't run. She could have, and no one would have gone after her. Maybe she was scared. Maybe she knew her best chance was with us. Or maybe she had different orders. If Florida wanted to crush the rebellion, all Tanya had to do was get rid of Quinn and I. Without us, the rest of the survivors would scatter to the wind.

It wouldn't take much in the tunnels. She could hide behind a rock on one of the corners, waiting for me, then fire a bullet right into my stomach. Yeah, the others would hear it, but she'd have plenty of time to get away before they figured out what happened. She could shoot Pam in the back. Then, when Quinn came back to see what was going on, she could shoot him in the head. She wouldn't get past me, but she would have inflicted extreme damage. My palms began to sweat and my heart rate increase. Why did I let her have a gun?

I watched her silhouette as we wound our way through the tunnels. I wished I could read minds, it would make everything so much easier. I hated not knowing what was going on. I hated not being able to tell Quinn, too. If anyone knew what to do with Tanya, it would be him.

Maybe I was being overly protective. It was possible I misjudged Quinn's reaction. I mean, he'd never done anything in the past to make me believe he would be extremely angry or hurt Tanya. But there was that night at the fire, and he barely spoke to her. He did blame her. It was best to play it safe. I couldn't risk pushing Quinn over the edge.

The scraping of wood against rock echoed through the tunnel. Quinn was attempting to move the makeshift barricade. It was difficult to see over the others in front of me, but I heard him grunting and struggling. The light flooded in. He successfully removed the blockade. I squinted and blinked at the light, moving forward with the rest until I stood amongst the trees. We formed a semi-circle with Quinn as our focus, waiting for instructions of what to do next. His back was toward us and he glanced through the trees, his hands over his eyes, shielding them from the sun.

"I think we can get to the complex over there." He pointed off to his right before turning to face us. "Keep a sharp look out. Last time we were through here, we ran into two undead. Who knows how many more are out there."

Pam nodded and pulled out her gun. I did the same. Tanya hesitated, but she also followed suit. I eyed her cautiously. Again, I hoped to bore my thoughts deep into her skull, warning her what would happen if she turned on any of us. She glanced at me briefly, then flicked her eyes to the ground.

Death To The Undead

Quinn headed off first, the rest of us flanking him. We stayed close together, within an arm's length. Sweeping outside was just like clearing a building, you didn't want to get too far away from each other, and you definitely didn't want to split up. That was a good way for someone to get shot. We stepped lightly, trying as best as we could not to make too much noise. Our footsteps crunched on dead leaves and gravel, as well as an occasional twig. Birds tweeted overhead. In the distance, a squirrel chattered. I glanced in the direction every time I heard a sound, but it also made me feel better to know animals were out. If there was trouble, they would have high-tailed it to safety. Zombies weren't known for their stealth abilities, and that distressed wildlife. I didn't know if a zombie would eat a bird or a squirrel, but I highly doubted either animal stayed around to find out.

We walked quite a ways through the trees. I scanned the area and listened for anything out of place, I didn't count steps. Eventually, we came to a chain link fence. If I hadn't seen it, I wouldn't have believed it. The trees didn't open into a clearing. There wasn't a logical reason for it to be there, but it encircled a large area of the forest. Signs posted at various intervals warned of electric shock, and razor wire adorned the top. To my left, a section had fallen down, or was maybe pushed over, it was hard to say. In the middle of it all was a small, metal shack. The trees hid it perfectly. If we hadn't of been looking for it, we wouldn't have found it. We all stopped and stared at the place in awe and confusion.

"What is this?" Pam asked.

I shrugged. "I have no idea."

"Well," said Quinn. "There's only one way we're going to find out. Let's head in."

He made his way toward the fallen part of the fence, and we all followed. We cautiously stepped over the fence, our senses heightened, the tension grew thicker. A bird flew between tree branches. I whipped around to stare at it. My stomach was in knots, my fingers tingled. To say I was uncomfortable in that area was an understatement. There was something creepy about the whole place, something I couldn't put my finger on. Who had a secret shack in the woods surrounded by a chain link fence? An electrified fence. Where did they get the power? And where were they now?

I knew the zombies we ran into days earlier had something to do with this place. But the way they were dressed, I knew it wasn't a hunting cabin. My brain told me to get out, to run far away, but my curiosity told me it was just a few steps further. I'd made it that far, might as well find out what was going on.

The four of us made it to the shack and stopped at the door. We looked at it, then at each other, then back at the sign on the door. It read: "Warning: Property of the United States Army. Trespassers will be shot on sight."

I took a deep breath. I knew whatever we were going to find behind the door wasn't going to be good.

Death To The Undead

CHAPTER 11

"It's just a scare tactic."

We all looked at Pam.

"I highly doubt the U.S. Army has anything to do with this place. I'm sure it's some crazy mountain guy who wants to be left alone."

"I don't know." My eyes scanned our surroundings again. "Why would he need an electric fence? And where would he get the power for it?"

Pam chuckled and shook her head. "You have no idea how insane some of these people are. I'm sure he has generators hooked up somewhere."

I knew how crazy survivalists could get. We had our share of them in Oregon before all this happened. Still, it didn't seem right. It seemed too high-tech, even for the most savvy of survivalists. I glanced around the trees. Hidden amongst the leaves were cameras, several of them pointed in our direction, while others stared onto the perimeter. Whoever owned the place didn't want anyone approaching without them knowing.

If it was the Army, though, I couldn't figure out how they got to the building. There weren't any roads, and it would be impossible to land a helicopter. It was possible they stopped in Dashton and hiked through the caves. Unless there was another opening somewhere else on the mountain. The building itself wasn't large. The four of us would be able to fit in it, but we'd have to stand shoulder to shoulder in sets of two. Whether it was the Army or some nut job, the place was easily defendable. I just wondered where they were.

"Try the door." Pam motioned with her gun. "See if it's unlocked."

Quinn stepped forward and turned the handle. The door popped silently open. Dang! I really hoped we wouldn't be able to get it. But I knew at the back of my brain I wasn't that lucky. The zombie had to come from somewhere, and I was convinced it was that place. A shard of sun illuminated a small portion of the building. I peeked in. A set of stairs angled down into darkness. Great. It couldn't just be a tool shed. Quinn glanced at us.

"I'll head down first. The rest of you stay close."

"Should one of us stay out here and keep guard?" Tanya asked.

Well, wouldn't that be convenient? It would make it much easier for her to run away. I wanted to say that, to snap at her for even suggesting such a thing, but I bit my tongue.

Quinn shook his head. "No, we all go together. If someone stays up here, and we all run out, someone might get shot."

She swallowed thickly, her head bobbing slightly. She tightened her grip on the gun. "Okay."

"You ready for this?" Quinn asked.

"No. But I'll be fine."

His jaw tightened and he took a deep breath. "Pam, you go behind me. Krista, keep an eye on Tanya."

He didn't have to tell me twice. I didn't plan on letting her too far out of my sight.

Quinn stepped through the door and down the stairs.

Pam followed behind, then Tanya. She hesitated, staring at me, her eyes glistened with fear. For a brief moment, I felt sorry for her. I remembered how scary the unknown was, how nerve-wracking it was to think we would run into a zombie. I pushed it down. I couldn't show empathy, especially after what she did to us. I jerked my head toward the stairs, encouraging her to go. She took a deep breath and headed in.

The air was cool. The faint stench of rot tickled my nose. The light from outside illuminated the first few steps, then we plunged into darkness. That was why we always kept flashlights on us. We never knew when we would be forced into some dark space, and we always wanted to be prepared. Quinn and Pam had theirs on, and I clicked mine on. I illuminated the walls. Boring, smooth concrete, and nothing else. No signs, no graffiti, no indication of what we headed into. I flexed my fingers around the handle of the gun and chewed on my lip.

Quinn's light disappeared. He must have reached the end of the stairs. I stepped onto the concrete floor with everyone else, and we shone our beams around the room. Again, concrete walls surrounded us. A single desk was on the right, and behind it, a short corridor to another door.

Pam stepped to her left and flipped a switch. Fluorescent lights flickered on, casting a sterile white glow into the room.

"Power's still on," Pam commented.

"Yeah. But where's it coming from?" I glanced at the others.

They shrugged as my eyes fell on them.

"I don't like this." Tanya's voice quaked.

I nodded. I didn't like it either.

"I don't think anyone is comfortable." Quinn tried to keep the irritation out of his voice, but a little crept through. "But we have to find out what we're dealing with here." He pointed to the door at the end of the hall. "Looks like our only option."

He stepped forward and grabbed the handle. Pam stood next to him, while Tanya and I had his back. Please don't let anything pop out of that door. Please.

Quinn made a silent count with his head, bobbing it three times before pulling open the door. Pam went low, pointing her gun through the opening. The door opened onto a larger room adorned with computer stations. The lights were already on, leading me to believe the switch controlled both rooms. They stepped through the door, scanning the room. Tanya and I waited at the door, ready to fire should anything pop out of a hiding place. Three computer stations lined the right and left sides in front of smaller rooms with windows. I swallowed thickly. They were observation centers. But what were they observing? I could only imagine. Pam and Quinn finished their sweep and holstered their weapons. Tanya and I did the same before stepping into the room. My thoughts drifted to what they did in that room. I remembered the conversation I had so long ago with the soldier on the back of the transport truck. He told me the civilians at the military base thought the government created the zombies. Could it be true? Did they use these rooms in their experiments? Did they put unsuspecting victims into the chambers, then turn them into zombies? Jotting down notes on their computers? It made sense to me. And it made my stomach churn.

Quinn stopped at the computer nearest the door and switched it on. The fan hummed to life, the screen blinked blue. He placed his hands on either side of the keyboard, waiting. We crowded around him. After a few minutes, the dialogue box asking for username and password popped onto the screen. Quinn sighed.

"Well, that's not going to do us much good. There's no way we're getting into this information."

I scanned the room. There had to be more. Files, papers, something. They couldn't trust technology to keep their information safe.

"Was there another room? Or is this it?"

"I didn't see another door," Pam answered.

Tanya circled the room, glancing through the windows, a look of distaste and confusion on her face.

"What do you think they kept in there?"

"I can only imagine," I murmured.

Death To The Undead

"Let's turn all of these on." Quinn gestured at the computers. "Maybe we'll get lucky and one will be logged on."

I cocked my head to the right and pursed my lips. It was a long shot. Most computers reset themselves after a long time, but what did we have to lose? I crossed the room and pushed the buttons to the three computers. The hum of the fans grew louder, though not overbearing. Tanya finished her gawking and pulled out a chair, plopping down in front of a computer. I sighed and folded my hands across my chest. I eyed her for a moment before stepping up to a window and glancing into the nearest room.

White tiles lined the walls and floor. A metal drain sat in the middle of the floor. Barren. Boring. Sterile. I walked to the other side of the room, the far wall opposite the door we came through. I leaned against the tiles.

"You're wasting your time," I told him. "We won't be able to access the computers."

A faint scraping, like gravel on gravel, sounded behind me, and I swear I felt the surface move. With eyebrows pushed together, I straightened up and stared at the wall. In the grout, there was a small crack. I squinted. It was too straight to be an accident. I stepped closer to the wall.

"Krista?" Quinn's voice sounded behind me. "What are you doing?"

I placed my hands on the tile and followed the line. Just as I suspected, it was the outline of a door. I looked at the others, pointing.

"There's a door here."

"A door?" Pam stepped forward.

"Is it a secret door?" Tanya wondered.

I pursed my lips and stared at her. A number of remarks ran through my head, but I decided to keep my mouth shut.

"Okay." Quinn stood next to me. "So how do we open it?"

"I don't know. But I swear I felt the wall move when I leaned against it."

Quinn placed his hands on the tiles and pushed. His face turned red, and small grunts escaped from his lips. The wall didn't move. He straightened up with a huff.

"I don't think it opens."

"It has to. There has to be other ways to access this place. How did they put whatever into those observation rooms?" I gestured toward the empty rooms with my good hand.

"I don't know what to tell you, Krista. I can't open the door."

"Then break through the tile," Pam suggested.

Quinn and I glanced at her for a moment.

"Good idea."

Quinn raced to the end of the room and disappeared out the door. The three of us waited for a moment, silent, wondering what he was doing. He returned a moment later with a rock in his hand.

Death To The Undead

The stone crunched against the wall, the thud reverberated through the room. Bits of dirt and small pebbles stuck to the tile. He smacked the wall again, harder. The rock fell to the ground. Quinn shook his hand, sucking in a sharp breath.

"Here." I reached around my neck and pulled the sling strap over my head. "Put it in here and swing it."

Quinn took the sling from me and secured the rock inside. Holding my wrist up with my other hand, I stepped back. I didn't want to get smacked.

Quinn swung the rock over his shoulder and into the wall. The thud was loud, followed by a sharp cracking sound. Lines appeared in the tile. He swung again. Part of the white wall collapsed inward. One more swing and he'd have a hole. The tile clinked onto the floor between the walls. He knelt down and stared through the hole.

"Yep. I see the handle. It's definitely a door."

Cautiously, he reached his hand through. After making a few faces and grunting, a click resounded, and the door swung open. We stared into the new dark room for a moment.

"Maybe we shouldn't go in there." Tanya's voice was quiet, shaky. "Maybe this door was secret for a reason."

I rolled my eyes. "I'm sure it was just a safety precaution. If the people weren't supposed to be able to go through it, why have it at all?" I unholstered my weapon.

"Here, take this back."

Quinn dumped the rock out of my sling. He attempted to brush the dirt fragments out, but I felt them on my skin when I placed my arm in. I'd worry about that later. Curiosity about what was in the other room was more pressing than a few pebbles digging into my flesh. I stepped forward.

The room was cooler than the other. Goosebumps formed on my skin. Sunlight streamed in from high above, lighting the opposite side of the opening in a gray hue. I clicked on my flashlight. The beam barely illuminated half the room. Actually, room might not be the best way to describe the place. Cave was more like it. The walls were rock, and the ceiling rose to a point. The floor was smooth concrete, but otherwise, we were in a mountain. The place was immense. I bet at least three helicopters and several Hummers could fit in there without touching each other, along with years worth of supplies. Our footsteps echoed eerily through the place. There wasn't much in there at the time. Did they take it all when the zombie attacks first started? Or was it never there to begin with?

The four of us glanced around the room. It wouldn't take long to sweep, there weren't too many places for anything to hide, although a few crates lined the far walls. Pam felt around the wall near the door. A click sounded, and sick orange lights clicked on. They barely illuminated the room, but it was better than nothing. Something scuttled to our right.

Death To The Undead

Instantly on high alert, we all spun around, guns up and ready. Quinn pointed at himself and Pam, then in the direction of the sound. They were going to check it out, Tanya and I were to stay behind. It didn't make me happy, but I nodded. The two slowly walked off.

A dragging, followed by a snort sounded. The hair on the back of my neck stood up, my muscles tensed. It could've been a dog, maybe another animal. It sounded like one. But how would they have gotten down there? And how would they have survived? It was wishful thinking, I knew that.

Quinn and Pam were within ten feet of the crates against the wall. Quinn signaled, indicating he was going to the right. Pam stopped, flanking his left side. He stepped up to the crate. The moan was loud, unearthly in the confined space. But it was nothing compared to the gun shot. My ears rang. Instinctively, I swung around and scanned the area behind Tanya and me to make sure no other creatures snuck up on us. I strained my ears, waiting for more creatures to emerge from the shadows, for us to be surrounded. My heart thumped in my chest. Moments passed. Nothing. I turned back to the others. Like me, they scanned the area, their guns pointed into the darkness, fingers itching to fire. Another moment passed. Still nothing. I relaxed slightly, taking a deep breath.

"I think we're clear," I said aloud. I cocked my head to the side and listened. If anything was going to draw out more zombies, it was speech.

Quinn nodded. "I think you're right. Come check this out."

I joined him by the crate and examined the body. Like the others, it was dressed in business wear. A white, button up shirt and gray pants. Clipped to his pocket was a badge. I stepped forward and grabbed it. Wiping off the blood, I read the writing. "He was a scientist." I told the others. "Dr. Stanson. Civilian position, but he did work for the Army." I handed the badge to Quinn.

"What is this place?" Tanya asked.

We all looked at each other, hoping someone had an answer, but no one did. Without being able to access the information in the computers, there was no way of knowing what went on in the cave.

"We don't really have time to worry about it." Quinn tossed the badge onto the floor. "Whatever went on here hasn't happened for years. Let's see if there's anything we can use and move on."

Pam and I nodded before heading off to check out crates.

"Tanya, why don't you come with me. I could use an extra hand," I said.

I still didn't want her getting too far out of my sight. Anything could happen in that cave, and anyone could escape undetected.

"Do you think they did something with zombies here?" Tanya wondered as we approached a crate. "I mean, those rooms seem so weird. Do you think they put infected people in there and studied them?"

"Tanya, honestly, I don't know. There is that possibility. But where are those people? If they did turn into zombies and infect the others here, where are they? We can speculate all we want, but we're never gonna know. In reality, we shouldn't waste our time. Here, help me with this lid."

We placed our hands on the top of the crate and pushed. With a scraping sound and squeak of wood, the top crashed onto the floor. I glanced in. I couldn't stop the smile from spreading over my lips.

"You've got to be kidding me!" I commented. It was a dream. It had to be. I reached into the box and pulled out an AR-15. The laugh wouldn't be contained. "Pam, Quinn. Check this out." I turned to show them the weapon.

Something slammed into my back, knocking me to the ground. Both guns slid across the floor. I gasped for air, pain exploded through my shoulder, fear gripped my chest. Panicked, I tried to roll over onto my back. I wasn't going to get bit without at least putting up a fight. Why hadn't the others shot? What were they doing? A hand grabbed the back of my hair and pulled me to my feet.

"Do something!" I screamed. "Help me!"

"You do, and she dies."

I knew that voice. My blood went cold. I risked turning my head. Out of the corner of my eye, I saw a familiar face.

"Liet." The name rushed out of my mouth in a breath. I couldn't believe what I actually said.

"Who were you expecting?" he snarled. "Another zombie?"

"I would have preferred one, yeah."

He tightened his grip on my hair and pulled me against his body. The barrel of a gun rested against my temple.

"I guess you're not that lucky," he hissed into my ear.

"Liet, come on now, let's be reasonable." Quinn held his hands out in front, talking calmly. "There are three of us and one of you."

"Oh, I'm well aware of that. And I have no doubt you'll kill me. But at least I'll take Krista down before you can get a shot off. I'll die happy knowing I took her away from you."

My throat tightened. He would do it. He was more than capable.

"Liet, we don't want that. I'm sure we can come to an understanding."

"Then I suggest you put your weapons on the ground. NOW!"

My head rattled as he yelled at the others. Tears threatened to fall. How did it come to this? Was this really happening? The others did as he commanded.

"Undo your arm sword." He practically yelled in my ear.

It took a moment, but I complied. It clanked onto the concrete floor.

"You," he gestured toward Tanya. "Stand with the others."

She raised her hands and side-stepped to be with Pam and Quinn. Liet moved the gun from the side of my head and pointed it at the others.

"Who wants to go first?"

"No!" I pleaded. "You have what you want. You have me. Let them go."

"They all deserve to die for what they did. Quinn it is."

The world was thrust into slow motion. Liet lined the gun up so it pointed at Quinn. His eyes went wide, and the barrel flashed. I pushed with all my might against Liet's body, hoping to make the bullet sail wide. Quinn's body jerked. He fell backward. Tanya and Pam took the opportunity and ran in opposite directions, looking for cover. Liet fired rapidly. I chopped the arm holding the gun.

"You brat!" He pointed the gun back at me. "This isn't over! They will get what's coming to them." He dragged me by my hair toward the door.

I stared at Quinn. Blood soaked the front of his shirt. He didn't move. Tears streamed down my face.

Liet dragged me up the stairs and outside. I pulled out of his grasp, not caring if I was missing a chunk of my hair. My intention was to claw his eyes out, get him to the ground, and pound his skull with a rock. He pointed the gun at my forehead.

"Try it. I dare you."

"Shoot me," I taunted. "You've already taken everything away from me."

A smile curled onto his lips. "That would be too easy. I have other plans for you. I'm taking you back to Florida."

He raised the gun and smashed it onto the side of my head. Blackness engulfed me.

Death To The Undead

CHAPTER 12

The sun sank behind the cliff face, streaking the sky and clouds a dark crimson. The horse shifted beneath me, snorting uncomfortably. I patted her neck and whispered soothing words.

"You sure nothing is down here?" I turned to Quinn.

"Of course."

"Then why are the horses so skittish?"

He shrugged. "Probably picking up on your vibes." He clicked his tongue, and his horse moved forward.

I stared after him, my eyes narrowed to slits. Why was he always so calm about things? Didn't he ever worry? How come I always had to be so high strung?

I pressed my heels into the animal's side, and she moved forward. Quinn was a ways in front of me, near the entrance to the canyon. He glanced over his shoulder and smiled. It put me at ease.

The rock walls surrounded him and his ride, casting them in shadows. A rumbling sounded, a low mumble that vibrated the ground. My horse stopped and jerked her head in the air, backing away from the canyon entrance. It started with a few pebbles, then, within seconds, larger rocks rolled down the canyon walls. Quinn glanced up, his eyes wide. He pulled the reins. The horse turned and started to run. Before he could make it out, the walls fell inward. Quinn was buried.

My chest hurt, my breath came in rasps. I screamed his name, but no sound came out of my mouth. I tired to get off the horse, but my foot tangled in the stirrup. She kept moving backward, the fear rose in her, the desire to run away overpowered her. I tried to keep the horse calm, attempted to say soothing things, but I couldn't. I didn't feel it.

Eventually, I got my foot untangled. As I was about to swing my leg over the saddle, the horse reared. I was thrown backward. Landing in the dirt with a thump, the air left my lungs. I gasped for breath. Darkness crept in. I had to get to Quinn before it was too dark to see. A hand appeared above me, reaching out to help me up. I didn't flinch. It never crossed my mind to wonder who else was out there with us. I grabbed it.

The fingers were cold and brittle. They jerked me to my feet with an unnatural strength. I lost my balance and fell forward, catching myself on the person's shoulders. The bones were prominent beneath the tattered shirt. My heart leapt into my throat. I knew I didn't want to, but I forced myself to look into the person's face.

Quinn's skull was crushed, his skin peeled down his cheeks. One eye was missing, the other dangled from the socket. He opened his mouth. Several teeth were gone, but he sunk the remaining ones into my neck. Again, I screamed, but no sound came out.

I jerked awake, sucking in a sharp breath. My head pounded, my shoulder was on fire, and the bright sun threatened to blind me. I moved my hand to rub my eyes, but it stopped short. Blinking rapidly, I glanced down. My hand was cuffed to the handle of a door. I squinted at my surroundings. Liet sat next to me, his hands on a steering wheel, his gaze focused forward. I felt groggy. Was I still dreaming? I tugged at the cuffs again.

"Knock it off," Liet growled. "They aren't going to come loose."

If I could focus and breathing didn't hurt, I would have lashed back at him, figured out a way to get my legs free and kicked him in the face, but I didn't have the energy.

"Where are we?" My mouth was dry, sticky, my throat sore. The words crackled out of my mouth.

"On our way back to Florida. Just like I told you."

The events from the cave rushed back into my mind. Quinn! Liet killed Quinn! Forget the headache and searing pain in my body, I needed to take him out. I moved my feet, calculating the best way to turn in my seat, when they stopped short. I tugged on them and glanced down. Twine. He secured my feet with twine. Well, you couldn't say Liet wasn't prepared.

"Aaaaah!" I screamed out of frustration and anger. I pulled and jerked and writhed against my restraints, hoping one of them would pop free.

Liet chuckled, a low, maniacal sound.

It sent me into a fit of rage. I did the only thing I could. I spit. It was more of a mist than an actual threat, but it accomplished its goal. Liet slammed on the brakes. I jerked forward in my seat. Luckily, Liet fastened my seatbelt. Not like I was going far with the other restraints, but it did prevent me from having a dislocated shoulder.

The tires squealed and burnt rubber tickled my nose. I was thrown back into my seat as the vehicle came to a complete stop. I thought Liet was going to tear the gear stick out of the side of the wheel. He turned in his seat, placed his hand on my neck, and stuck his face inches from mine. He pushed my head into the headrest.

"It's going to be a very long trip to Florida. I suggest being on your best behavior."

"Or what?" I snarled. "There is nothing left you can do to hurt me. You've taken away everything."

"Trust me, Krista." His voice was low. "There are worse things than death."

I scoffed. "Like what? Being a zombie? I'm pretty sure wandering the earth with nothing on my mind but flesh would be a blessing right now. The only thing that would suck is I wouldn't remember to come after you!"

He tightened his grip on my neck. The air barely made it into my lungs. My headache increased.

Without saying a word, he released me and put the vehicle in drive. I had him. I knew it. There was nothing he could do to me. The one thing I wanted was for him to kill me. It would save a lot of heartache. Yeah, the people in Florida still needed me, but the mission seemed hollow without Quinn to help. Tears stung my eyes, but I refused to let them fall. I averted my gaze out the window.

Death To The Undead

Liet found a Hummer, more than likely outside the Army cave. I attempted to look over the seat, see what he packed in the back. From the corner of my eye, I saw dark green duffel bags and a stack of guns. Liet was smart enough to know he'd need food and water, but he also needed to take something to appease The Families. No doubt they were going to be angry the workers took over North Platte. They were probably upset they had to come out and level the whole place. They were going to be furious to know they didn't actually kill any of the uprisers in the attack. Liet had a lot of explaining to do, but he could smooth the way with a gift.

Liet. Even thinking his name made me nauseous. Why had we shown him mercy? Why didn't we string him up on the barbed wire fence in North Platte and let the zombies take care of him? We wanted to lead by example, show how compassionate we were. You know, the complete opposite of Liet. But what did that accomplish? Quinn got shot, and I was kidnapped. Plus, he knew where the survivors were. He could send out an extermination crew once we got to Florida. I could only hope Pam and Tanya got back to camp and told them to move out.

I clenched my jaw. What else could possibly go wrong? Lately, it seemed like everyone I ran into wanted to kill me. My luck ran out. It was the only explanation. It had to happen sooner or later, but why couldn't it have been after the siege on Florida? Maybe during the victory party I could randomly get struck by lightning.

"Life doesn't work like that, Krista." I heard my father's voice in my head. "Rome wasn't built in a day."

I punched the car door, frustrated. There's nothing I could do about my situation. I was stuck. Dad would say, "There's always a way. You might not see it, but you're never truly stuck." Obviously, that man had never been handcuffed inside a car with a lunatic.

"You know, Krista." Liet's voice was soft, kind.

I focused my glare on him, just to make sure it was actually Liet in the car.

"It's not too late to fix things between us."

My jaw dropped open. He was joking. He had to be. He glanced at me.

"What?" His voice had a hint of anger to it.

"Did you do drugs as a child?"

"What?"

"How else do you want me to ask it? It's a straight forward question."

"Yeah. Some."

"That probably explains a lot." I turned my attention back out the window.

"Whatever. Either way, we're still family. The only we have left. With Quinn gone, you have no one left. Except me."

I balled my hand into a fist. Did he really believe I was going to run back to him after he shot Quinn? Was he really that narcissistic? I decided not to respond. I wouldn't have been able to say anything nice.

"If you come back, I'll make sure The Families go lenient on you."

I snorted and faced him. "You'd still take me down there?"

"What other choice do I have? You broke the rules. You have to pay the consequences. But I can make sure you aren't killed for what you've done."

"Really?" I made my voice rise unnaturally high. "You'd do that for me? Oh, Liet, I don't deserve you."

He glanced at me sideways.

"You can shove it up your butt!" I snarled. "I've never needed you to do me any favors."

His lip curled into a snarl. "Fine. Suit yourself. I was trying to give you one more chance."

I rolled my eyes, but he didn't see it.

I slouched down into my seat, turning my back on him as best as I could. I wanted to spend the rest of the trip in silence. It would take days for us to get to Florida. Not talking to him would make it slightly bearable.

"So, what do you think went on in the Army base?"

Thank goodness Liet's split personalities could still come out and play. It wouldn't be a family gathering without everybody there.

I didn't respond.

"I think they studied zombies there. Maybe created them."

"Then where were they?"

"What do you mean?"

"I mean, if they studied the undead or even created them, wouldn't there be some kind of evidence? Wouldn't the creatures still be in the cells? They couldn't get out of those rooms."

"What do you think happened?"

"I don't know, Liet. I wasn't there. You were in there longer than we were, what did you find?"

"Nothing but those crates of guns. And a few roaming zombies. All civilians. No military people."

"Then I guess we'll never know what happened."

"That place is kind of like area fifty-one, isn't? Buried deep in the mountain, unknown to the vast majority of people. Anything could have gone on in there."

"Maybe it was a safety shelter. You know, like Cheyenne Mountain."

Liet sat quietly for a moment. "Maybe. But I didn't see any living quarters in there."

"Then maybe it was just a storage facility. Maybe they were going to take creatures there but never had the chance. Maybe they turned before they could get the zombies imprisoned."

"It would make sense. I mean, you'd want to make sure you were stocked to the gills with weapons before bringing in a dangerous creature. It would also explain the few civilians. They're probably the ones who left this baby there." He patted the steering wheel. "Not that I'm complaining."

"Are you done speculating? I have a huge headache. I'd like to rest."

"Oh, sure. Sorry. I forgot I whacked you pretty hard with my gun. When I stop for a break, I'll get you something for that."

I responded by getting as comfortable as I could and closing my eyes. The pain subsided slightly, almost to a tolerable level. I tried not to think about my situation. I didn't want to think about Liet and his twisted idea of family and the actions he thought he needed to do to accomplish his goal. I especially didn't want to think about Quinn because I knew I couldn't keep my emotions in check forever. The last thing I wanted was for Liet to know he hurt me. If anyone was going to get hurt, it was going to be him. I didn't know how or when I was going to do it, but I was going to do it.

The tires vibrated and sound rumbled through the Hummer. I opened my eyes as Liet pulled over onto the side of the road.

"Where are we?"

"I don't know. Somewhere in Colorado, I think. I need a break, though. And I'm sure you could use some water."

He opened the door and walked to the back. He returned a few minutes later and held out a bottle of water and two ibuprofen.

"Are you kidding? How do you expect me to take that?"

"Oh, yeah." He placed the pills into my right hand, then turned the top of the bottle. "You'll have to bend down."

"Or you can undo the cuffs."

Liet chuckled. "Yeah, right. You're resourceful. You'll figure it out." He took a swig of his own water.

I stared at him, hard, hoping he would burst into flames. Sadly, he didn't, and I desperately needed water. I lifted my hand as high as I could, then bent my head to meet it. It probably didn't look pretty, but I accomplished my goal. Liet finished his water before tossing the plastic bottle onto the ground. He climbed back into his seat and headed down the road.

"What do you plan on doing with me when I have to pee?"

Liet smiled. "I guess we'll figure that hurdle out when we get to it."

I had half an inclination to flip the rest of my water at him, then throw the bottle, but I knew if I did, he'd take water away from me completely. Eventually, I'd need my strength. And I read before that dying from dehydration was a horrible way to perish. Even more torturous than having to spend days in a car with Liet. If nothing else, I could pee my pants. Yeah, it'd be miserable, but it would make Liet miserable too. I wasn't completely defeated.

Death To The Undead

CHAPTER 13

It took us four days to get to Florida. And trust me, they were the longest, most intolerable days ever! Nice Liet was present for the trip. That helped a little. He even let me pee on my own. However, he never untied my feet, and I only had one hand to undo my pants. It would have been better if I peed my pants.

We ate and slept in the Hummer, so every muscle in my body ached. My shoulder was the worst of everything, and I was concerned it wouldn't heal properly. Liet's tackle didn't help. I needed a doctor, piece of mind, but who knew if Liet would let me see one. I could've played nice, pretended like I wanted to be a family again, then I'm sure I could've asked for a checkup, but I couldn't do it. Just the thought of it made my skin crawl and my stomach cramp. He didn't deserve my worst acting skills.

All the pain and anguish I felt over Quinn's death hardened into hate and revenge and settled into the center of my chest. I didn't care about compassion or how future generations would look at me, I wanted Liet dead. And I wanted to kill him.

I sat uncomfortably in the seat, attempting to take a nap. What else was I going to do? If Liet thought I was asleep, he wouldn't talk to me. I resolved myself to my fate. The Families' anger would be satiated with my death, I knew that. Plus, I'd become an example. I imagined how they would sensationalize my case. It would strengthen their control over the masses. I didn't care. I had nothing left to fight for. It was a hopeless mission we set ourselves on anyway.

Liet slowed the Hummer, and I opened my eyes. Florida's chain link border was directly in front. The guards flanked the side of the road, guns at the ready. Thank goodness, I thought. My time with Liet was close to an end. A jail cell was going to be heaven.

Liet stopped and rolled down the window. He placed his arm on the door, taking on an air of nonchalance. The guard stepped forward, his face scrunched with seriousness.

"What is your business in Florida?" His eyes scanned the vehicle. Confusion covered his face as he glanced at me. He opened his mouth to speak, but recognition sparked when he looked at Liet. "General Liet!" he breathed. "We thought you were dead."

The smirk on Liet's face flipped into a frown. Red crept up his neck. "Why would I be dead? I can handle a few upstarts."

"Uh, yeah, right." The guard straightened up. "Of course you can, sir." He signaled to the others behind him. "Give us a minute, we'll give you an escort to Johnsons' Town."

I snorted in distaste. Of course Mrs. Johnson renamed the town. How many other places had been renamed? The guard raised his eyebrows and stared at me for a moment. I rolled my eyes and looked away. Two topless Jeeps took positions in front and behind us. Large machine guns were secured to the roll bars. Strings of bullets hung out of the side, like disemboweled intestines. Really? They needed that much fire power? I guess keeping the humans in line in Florida was a tough job. Or maybe they were trying to keep the rest of us out.

Quinn and I and the rest of the Westerners could have done so much with a weapon like that. We could've cut through a whole herd of undead. Oh, well. Too late to change it. Why worry about it?

"Looks like we're ready to go, sir." The guard pulled me out of my thoughts. "If you want, I can drive you into Johnsons' Town. Give you some rest, sir."

"Yeah. I'd like that." He turned to me. "Looks like you'll be riding in the back." He flashed a smile.

I scowled and looked over the seat. The only places to sit were two fold downs chairs. They weren't going to be comfortable. But Liet wasn't concerned with my well being.

Liet made sure my handcuff was secured to something on the underside of the seat before putting on my seatbelt. Another guard sat across from me. Liet wasn't taking any chances. After everyone was loaded, we passed through the gate into Florida. I stared at the fence until it faded from view. I settled into the seat as well as I could and closed my eyes.

"It's really nice to see you alive, sir," the driver said. "We were told to expect the worst. We thought the rebels might try to attack us."

Liet chuckled. "You don't have to worry about the rebels." He spit the word out like it left a bad taste on his tongue. "They aren't even close to being a threat."

I opened my eyes and tried to shoot lasers into the back of his head.

"That's good to know, sir. I'm sure The Families will be happy to hear it, too."

The vehicle drifted into silence. After a few minutes, snores sounded from the front. Liet fell asleep.

"When's the last time you saw a zombie?" I asked the soldier across from me. She didn't look much older than me, maybe a couple of years.

"You don't have to answer, Private." The driver's voice was low, authorial. "You can make the prisoner shut up."

Again, I tried to make lasers shoot out of my eyes into the back of his head.

"It's all right, sir. She's not bothering me." She focused her gaze on me. "It's been a while. I bet you've seen a lot."

I shrugged. I wasn't trying to make friends, I was just sick of silence. Besides, any voice other than Liet's was more than welcome.

"It varies from day to day, but there's never a dull moment. Lots of opportunity to keep my skills sharp and use my brain. Every day is an adventure filled with excitement."

She looked at me skeptically. "What's the most zombies you've ever killed at one time?"

Death To The Undead

I could've made up a story, made myself into a heroine, but what was the point? I'd been through and seen a lot. I'd faced down and killed more zombies than I could count. I could've told her about International Falls or about the gauntlet we had to run to get into North Platte or even about the hordes that roamed the highways, but she wouldn't have believed me. She would probably politely nod, all the while cursing me in her mind as a liar. I didn't need her approval or awe.

I smiled. "You wouldn't believe me if I told you."

She pursed her lips. "I might. We've heard stories down here. Are there really millions of creatures?"

"Probably worldwide. No one knows how many there are here. No one's taking the time to study them."

"Why would we study them?" The driver didn't attempt to keep the contempt out of his voice.

I shot a dirty look at the back of his head. "You're not the least bit curious where they came from? What caused them to be zombies? Is it a virus? Bacteria? Can they be cured?"

The Hummer sat in silence for a moment.

"Even if we don't study them, why isn't something being done about them?" I interrupted the quiet. "Why do the humans have to cower in Florida while the zombies roam free on our land?"

Liet adjusted in his seat and cleared his throat. After a few minutes, the snoring resumed. I leaned my head back on my seat.

"I guess complacency is easier than taking a stand. I guess being told what to do is easier than thinking for yourself. I wouldn't know. I've been out there, trying to make a difference." I cocked my head to the right. "Is it easier?"

"I do my part." Her tone was defensive.

I nodded. "Sure you do." I directed my attention to the driver. "What about you Captain Butt Kiss? Does complacency and moronicy make life easier?"

"This conversation is over. Private, refrain from talking to the prisoner."

I smiled and focused my gaze out the back window.

***

Our menagerie drew quite a crowd at the high school. Of course, I'm sure watching me shuffle by with my tied legs, handcuffed to Liet, and surrounded by armed guards was the most exciting thing the kids had seen in a while. It gave them something to talk about other than who was dating who and what outfit they were going to wear the next day. I glanced back at the gawkers, a smile on my face. I'm sure they thought I was insane. I'm sure they wandered why I didn't walk with my head hanging low, ashamed of what I'd done, defeated. Oh, if they only knew the truth. Poor, brainwashed sheep.

We walked into the school, past the front desk, and headed directly into the elevator. Four of us made the trip up: me, Liet, Captain Butt Kiss, and the soldier who sat across from me in the Hummer. I called her Private Lamb Chop in my mind, she reminded me so much of that puppet. Plus, if she ever did run into a zombie, she probably would get slaughtered.

Mrs. Johnson wouldn't be surprised to see us. The minute we stepped through the door, someone was on the phone informing her of our approach. As the lights for each floor lit up, I chuckled to myself. I imagined Mrs. Johnson scurrying to prepare for our arrival, yelling orders at the servants, clapping her hands to hurry them up. But when we walked through the door, she'd be sitting on the couch, like she'd been lounging all day.

The door dinged open and we stepped into the hallway. Mrs. Johnson's bodyguard, the same one who made the trip to North Platte and put zombies in the back of the semi, stood in front of the suite door, smirking at me. He thought he was so superior, like he single-handedly brought our rebellion to an end. I contemplated spitting on him as I walked by, but why give him the satisfaction of knowing he got to me? Instead, I put on the cheesiest, sweetest smile I could muster.

"I see Liet got his justice," the bodyguard commented as he opened the door.

"Maybe. But I'm still alive."

The man chuckled. "Probably not for long."

I shrugged. "Until then."

We stepped into the suite. As I suspected, Mrs. Johnson rose from the couch to greet us.

"General Liet! It is such a pleasure to see you alive." She held out her hands to him but stopped short, delicately covering her nose with her fingertips.

"Sorry," Liet apologized. "It's been a while since I've had running water."

She waved her hand through the air. "I understand. Perhaps we should postpone this meeting until you've had a chance to freshen up."

"With all due respect, ma'am, I'd like to have a decision made about Krista now."

Mrs. Johnson stared at me, hard, her lips pressed into a thin line. "She could stand a shower, too. And a doctor should look her over."

Liet stared from her to me and back again. "You can't be serious! She doesn't deserve special treatment!"

Mrs. Johnson folded her arms across her chest. "Do you want to risk making her a martyr? We have a delicate balance of power and sympathy down here, General. There are those who could use her mistreatment to their advantage. I will not give them fuel for their fire. If you don't like my method, you should have taken care of her yourself when you had the chance."

Liet scowled, his face turned red. "I still have that option."

She huffed. "I dare you to try it. She's in our possession now."

Liet leaned forward. "What are you going to do? You still need someone on the outside, someone who knows where the others are."

Mrs. Johnson pursed her lips. "Assuming we're going to waste our time looking for the other survivors. They're gone. What do we have to worry about?"

"They hid next to a cave, an old Army base. There are crates of guns in there. You really want to risk them coming down here?"

She waved her hand through the air. "We can take care of them, we outnumber them. There's no way they'll come down here."

"You don't know. They might."

"Liet," Mrs. Johnson had an edge to her voice. "We can take care of ourselves down here. We've been doing it for years. I'm not discounting what you've done for us, but you have no say in the day-to-day activities of Florida. That is The Families' job."

Liet scowled. "You wouldn't be here if it weren't for me. You would have been overthrown years ago. I took care of your problems."

Mrs. Johnson clicked her tongue. "Yes. We all know how well that worked out."

Liet's face took on a purple hue. "I could have left them here. Then, where would your delicate balance of sympathy and power be? In your own uprising? Dealing with your own rebels? Be thankful there are just a handful of them you have to deal with, and they're kids."

"I'm well aware of what could have happened were you not willing to take the rabble to North Platte. But you must realize, you're no longer in North Platte, you're in my town. Different rules govern down here, and you are expected to follow them just like everyone else."

Liet opened his mouth to speak but was interrupted.

I laughed. I couldn't help it. Seeing the two of them fight like children was the best show I'd seen in weeks. It was better than a soap opera. Both Mrs. Johnson and Liet glared at me in anger. It was never a good idea to show weakness in front of your enemy, and that's exactly what they did. There was a power struggle between the two, one that could easily be exploited. Liet scared Mrs. Johnson, I saw it in her eyes. But she didn't want him to know. Like he didn't already. He couldn't do anything, though. Mrs. Johnson had bodyguards and soldiers to back her up if Liet tried to harm her, so he had to be on his best behavior, much to his distaste. If given enough time, those two would probably destroy each other. Too bad we didn't have more time, it would have been an entertaining show.

She signaled to her bodyguard. "Take her to the hospital."

Reluctantly, Liet undid his side of the handcuff and slapped it onto the other man's wrist. I glanced at Liet over my shoulder and pushed out my bottom lip.

"Should've shot me after taking care of Quinn."

He pointed at me. "There's still a chance I can take care of you."

I smiled and nodded. "Sure there is."

The bodyguard jerked on my wrist. I turned to head out the door and ran into Pearl.

"Krista?" she squeaked. "What's going on?" Tears moistened her eyes.

The man pulled me into the elevator.

"Don't worry, Pearl. Everything is going to be all right."

The door slid shut as a tear dropped onto her cheek. I knew she didn't believe me, but what else could I say? I knew it wasn't going to be all right, but I was fine with my fate. I welcomed it.

CHAPTER 14

The best part about being a prisoner of The Families was I didn't have to wait to be seen by a doctor. We walked into the hospital and went straight to x-ray.

"I'll need you to remove the sling and your shirt," the nurse said matter-of-factly.

I stared at the bodyguard and held up my wrist. "You gonna help me out here?"

He scowled and unlocked my side before folding his arms across his chest. I lifted the sling strap over my head.

"You gonna watch me undress too?"

He clicked his tongue and walked to the door. Luckily, Private Lamb Chop came with us. She stepped into the room and took over babysitting duties.

It took less than ten minutes to have x-rays done, and then I was placed in an examination room to wait for the doctor. The bodyguard reattached our wrists and stood next to me, scowling. He glanced at his watch several times and sighed.

"Must be such a waste of your time," I told him. "I'm sure you would rather be killing innocent people."

"What?"

In my opinion, there should have been more shock in his voice, but he actually sounded more bored than anything.

"I know about the zombies," I whispered. "The ones you planted in the supply truck after your visit to North Platte."

Death To The Undead

He smiled and leaned forward, matching his volume with mine. "Good luck proving that."

The door opened and the doctor stepped in. He placed my x-ray on the light board.

"Things look pretty good. Some of your screws shifted, which might cause slight deformation when the bone heals completely, but it won't hinder your shoulder function." He stepped to me and lifted my shirt. "No sign of infection. That's good. But these stitches are way over due for removal." He stepped in front of me. "I'll get you some pain pills and send in the nurse. You'll have to wear your sling for six weeks, and try to refrain from physical activity. Anything else you need me to look at? Maybe this nasty lump on the side of your head?"

"The lump's fine. It'll heal faster than my shoulder. But I seem to have a strange growth on my wrist." I held up the handcuffs. "I think it might be cancerous."

The doctor wasn't amused. He nodded curtly before leaving the room. The nurse came in a few minutes later to remove my stitches.

The ride to the jail was uncomfortable. My skin was prickly and itchy from the threads being pulled out. Plus, I was tired. I may have slept a lot in the Hummer, but it was far from restful. I looked forward to a shower and a real bed. I also looked forward to leaving my present company. They bored me. I wanted to be alone.

Private Lamb Chop took me directly to the showers. She undid the handcuffs and cut off the twine around my ankles. The bodyguard rubbed his wrist and scowled at me.

"Let me know if she gives you any trouble," he told the private before leaving the room.

With some difficulty, I stripped out of my clothes. She handed me a mini shampoo and tiny bar of soap.

"I'll get you a towel and change of clothes."

"This isn't enough," I told her. "I need at least two more."

She scowled as she examined me. I could only imagine what ran through her mind. I knew I was dirty. I spent four days in a truck. Before that, we camped in the woods and traipsed through caves. Fresh water wasn't a luxury to be used for bathing. Eventually, she slapped more toiletries into my hand.

I stepped into the concrete shower. The smell of mildew drifted in the air, and a shower dripped at the far end with a plink-plink sound. The floor was slick under my feet. The water turned on with a squeak of the handle. The warmth felt like heaven on my skin, and a layer of dirt washed down the drain.

My mind drifted to Quinn. I fought back the tears forming in my eyes. How could this have happened? How could we have been so stupid to walk into a trap? No, stop it. We didn't know Liet was in that cave. How could we? It was circumstance, that's it. Still, there had to have been something I could've done. Maybe fought harder, pushed against Liet sooner. I couldn't hold the tears back. I broke down in sobs, my legs weakened, my knees buckled. I crouched on the floor, sobbing uncontrollably. If only we'd taken care of Liet when we had the chance. I sucked in a deep breath. I couldn't worry about it, I shouldn't. I couldn't change it. I did my best. Still, it didn't make me feel better. I cried until I was physically exhausted and couldn't produce anymore tears.

I could barely keep my eyes open when I stepped out and grabbed the towel from the private. I put on my bright orange shirt and pants, along with my sling, and followed her to my cell.

"You're being kept in holding cells," she explained, "away from the general population. They're afraid you might insight a riot. But don't worry, you won't be alone."

I found it odd she felt the need to explain to me about my accommodations. What was the big deal? They could put me anywhere they wanted. I wasn't going to talk to anyone, I was going to sleep. I didn't care about liberating Florida anymore. There wasn't anything left to fight for.

Private Lamb Chop stopped in front of a cell, and the door slid open with a buzz and clang of metal.

"Krista?" The voice sounded behind me.

I turned. Bill stood from his bed and approached the bars, his eyes wide.

"Krista!" His brother was in the cell next to him. He had a little more enthusiasm in his voice. He also approached the door.

Great, just what I needed. No doubt they thought I was there to save them. How could I tell them all hope was lost? How could I tell them they sacrificed themselves for nothing? I felt ashamed and helpless, like a failure. It was one thing to deal with the pain internally. When it was just Liet and I, I could forget about the others, withdraw inside my own mind, pretend no one else existed. I couldn't ignore or forget the boys when they were right in front of me. I couldn't pretend I was the only one the events affected. I averted my gaze to the floor and stepped into my cell with head hanging low. I flopped onto the cot and placed my forehead against the wall. They whispered across the hall.

"What's going on? Why didn't she talk to us?" I couldn't tell which brother it was.

"She's tired. It's been a long journey. Let her rest. I'm sure she'll talk to us when she gets up."

Oh, I was sure I'd have to talk to them. I didn't have anywhere to go, and trying to avoid them would raise suspicion. But what exactly was I going to tell them? It became painfully apparent that I was going to have to tell the guys Quinn was dead. Could I say those words out loud? They'd want to know the story. Would they blame me? I pushed the thoughts out of my head. I'd deal with it when I had to. I needed rest. I settled into the pillow and closed my eyes.

***

Death To The Undead

Quinn and I stood on the roof of the jail in Casper. Black clouds covered the sky, with hints of red on the horizon. The wind blew, drowning out all sound and making it difficult to stand upright. Quinn told me something, I watched his mouth move, but couldn't hear him.

"What?" I barely heard my own voice.

A strong gust pushed against my chest, my feet slid across the gravel rooftop. Instinctively, I reached for Quinn. Another rush of air pushed me farther back. Quinn grabbed my hand, but we didn't stop. The momentum took us to the edge of the roof.

The backs of my legs hit the short wall that surrounded the top of the building. My back arched, my arms flailed. I glanced over my shoulder. A sea of zombies reached for me. Millions of them, undulating like waves. The wind subsided, and I regained my balance. I turned to look at Quinn. He was no longer in front of me, no longer had a hold of my wrist. He teetered on the edge of the building, leaning precariously over the edge. I reached for him. Too late. He fell over the side. His body hit the creatures. He reached for me before slowly sinking beneath the rotted hands and snapping teeth. I screamed, but my voice was lost on the wind.

Another gust slammed into my back, pushing me over the edge. The creatures rushed toward me. I closed my eyes and brought up my hands to brace for impact.

I sucked in a sharp breath and jerked awake. Tentacles of pain snaked through my entire body. I groaned.

"Krista?" The voice drifted across the hall. Which brother was that? "You all right?"

Maybe if I didn't answer, he'd think I was still asleep. I closed my eyes. The sea of zombies waited in my mind's eye. Maybe I'd take my chances with Bill and Kyle. I moved to the edge of the bed.

"Yeah," I croaked. "I'm okay."

I moved to the sink in the corner of the room and turned on the faucet. A trickle of water came out. I frowned. I peed more than that. I shrugged and splashed my face several times before heading to the door, wiping the wetness on my sleeve.

Kyle's elbows rested on the cross bars, his hands folded in the hallway. He acted totally nonchalant. Bill had his hands on his hips, his eyebrows pushed together. They wore the same orange outfit as I, and their faces were a little pale from not being in the sun. Otherwise, they looked fine. They might have even put on a little weight. It's amazing what non-canned food can do.

"What happened to your arm?" Bill wondered.

I glanced at the sling, like I noticed it for the first time. "Liet shot me. Broke my shoulder blade."

"Are you all right?" Kyle sounded concerned.

It was one of those stupid questions to ask. Of course I wasn't all right! I'd been shot, my shoulder was broken, I had limited mobility in my arm. Plus, after seeing the doctor in Florida, I apparently was going to be deformed. Stupid as the question was, it was socially polite to ask. I contemplated giving him a sarcastic response, I was still tired and grumpy, but thought better of it. No need to take my frustrations out on him, he was just being nice.

"I'll survive this," I responded.

Bill stepped forward and grabbed the bars. "So what's the plan? Is the rest of the posse on their way?"

"Yeah," Kyle chimed in. "How are we gonna get out of here?"

A lump developed in my throat. "We're not."

Bill's brow furrowed deeper. "What do you mean? Why are you here then?"

I took a deep, shaky breath. "Liet captured me and brought me here to pay for my crimes."

They stared at me, waiting for an explanation. I told them everything that happened after we split up in Wyoming. They listened intently, the worry and concern deepening the wrinkles on their foreheads.

"Liet surprised us in the cave. He grabbed me and uh...he, um..." The words stuck in my throat. Tears involuntarily fell from my eyes. "He shot Quinn."

The brothers stared at me in disbelief. I couldn't stop the tears, my breathing came in rasps. Every inch of my body ached from Quinn's loss. I wanted to curl into the fetal position and ball up so tight I would disappear.

"Was he dead?" Kyle's voice was soft.

Another one of those questions. I nodded.

"There was blood everywhere, and he wasn't moving."

Kyle bit his lip and lowered his head.

"What about the others?" Bill's tone was serious, unemotional. "They still coming for us?"

I stared at him. Had he heard anything I just said?

"Why would they come after us? It's over. There's nothing left to fight for."

Bill huffed. "It's not over. We still have a job. People to liberate."

I wiped away my tears, the sadness once again hardened into anger. "These people don't want to be saved. They're happy living like sheep. We've already given so much, and what have they done in return?"

"They're not happy, Krista. They're brainwashed and scared. We're the only ones who can do anything"

"How?" My voice was on the edge of yelling. "Quinn's dead and we're in jail. More than likely, they're going to execute us. And what do I care if these people are happy or not? Do I look like a fairy godmother?"

"C'mon, Krista. There's always a way. Figure something out."

I leaned my head against the bars. "What's the point?"

"Because Quinn would have wanted it that way."

I clicked my tongue on the roof of my mouth in irritation. "Quinn doesn't have to worry about it now. And neither should we."

Kyle shook his head. "C'mon, Krista. Don't talk like that. The world isn't that bleak."

Death To The Undead

I scoffed. "Isn't that bleak? Have the weeks in here made you forget?" I pressed my face through the bars. "It's not only the zombies who want to kill you out there." I pointed at the door, "It's the humans too."

"We know," Bill said flatly. "Tanya's the one who put us in here."

I dropped my hand to my side. "I know. She told me."

Kyle's eyes widened. "You talked to Tanya?"

I sighed. "She found us in North Platte. Then, after we abandoned the city and headed to the mountains, she confessed everything."

"What did you do to her?" Bill's voice was low.

"Nothing. There wasn't time."

He let out a sigh. I didn't know if it was a sigh of relief or disappointment.

"It's not worth it." I continued. "All the betrayal and murdering, what's the point in helping others? We need to forget them and focus on ourselves."

"Not everyone is like that, Krista." Bill stepped closer to the bars. "There is still good in the world. You can't fight for what's right without sacrifice."

I pushed myself away from the door. "I'm tired of making sacrifices. I don't want to fight for what's right. Let them fend for themselves."

"You don't mean that, Krista." Kyle's voice was soothing. "You're grieving. Think about what Quinn would want, what he'd do."

I huffed and headed to my cot. What did they know? They didn't know how I felt, what I was going through. They didn't know what I'd given up, the things I'd lost. Or did they?

Death To The Undead

CHAPTER 15

Quinn, Bill, and Kyle knew about sacrifice. They'd done more for the country, for strangers in North Platte, and for me than anyone I'd ever known. They didn't have to answer Liet's initial call. They could've stayed on the ranch, living out their lives, ignoring the rest of the world. They weren't bothered by zombies, so why should they care about a few ingrates who refused to take care of the problem?

Bill was right. Quinn wouldn't have wanted me to give up. He would've wanted me to fight to the end. But he should've been standing right next to me, supporting and fighting with me. How was I supposed to do it on my own?

Why couldn't Liet have shot Pam? Or Tanya for that matter. If anyone deserved to die, it was her. Ungrateful, back-stabbing traitor! But their deaths wouldn't have upset me as much. Liet didn't have a personal vendetta against them. He'd wanted to kill Quinn for a long time. I hate that he got his chance. And, technically, if given the chance, he would have shot Pam and Tanya too. He didn't have time.

Quinn's death made me think of my parents, but his murder was totally different from theirs. All three of them were unexpected, but at least Quinn wasn't doing something stupid. We were all in the cave, trying to figure out what it was for, how were we supposed to know Liet used it as a hiding place? I told my parents it was dangerous to go to the military base, but they didn't listen. They walked into trouble and deserved what they got. Quinn was a victim of circumstance.

The pain from Quinn's death was intense, but it wasn't nearly as deep as when my parents were killed. Yes, they deserved it, and yes, it made me angry, but I knew them longer. They raised me, took care of me. They were my parents for crying out loud! Quinn was just a guy I met that I recently started dating. I wanted to get to know him better, I probably could have fallen in love with him, but that time had passed. I'd never get the chance. And I couldn't change it.

Was I being callous? Uncaring? Maybe. It's not that I didn't miss him, I did. I was sad he was killed, but not devastated. It was the way of life in zombie-infested lands. People were killed or turned into the undead. I had to get used to that. I shed my tears for him, and I'd probably shed more. The best way to honor his memory was to finish what he started. Save the people of Florida. No matter how much they didn't deserve it and would probably resent us for it.

I got up from the cot and headed back to the door, placing my hand on the bars. "If you have any ideas of what we could possibly do to get out of here, I'm listening."

Bill shook his head. "I have no clue."

I clenched my jaw. "So, you're just hoping something will happen?"

"Liet had every opportunity to kill you, and he didn't. Maybe we can use that to our advantage."

Death To The Undead

"There has to be a way, Krista," Kyle interjected. "It can't end like this."

I opened my mouth to speak, but was interrupted by a door opening. Private Lamb Chop stepped into the hallway and approached my cell.

"Mrs. Johnson would like to see you."

"They didn't send you back to the border?" It was more of an observation than a question.

A small smile covered her lips. "General Liet personally requested I stay on as your guard." A hint of red crept into her cheeks.

My stomach knotted. I should've said something to warn her, tell her about his mood swings and multiple personalities, but, again, she wouldn't have believed me. She would have assumed I was making things up, telling her lies because I was a prisoner, because I had a bad experience with Liet. Best to let her find out on her own.

"Oh, how nice for you." It was the only response I thought of.

She looked at me sideways. My tone had a bit of cynicism in it. Thank goodness she picked up on it.

The door buzzed and slid open. She held out the handcuffs, and I let her snap it around my wrist. She clicked the other side onto her arm.

"You know," I observed, "it's awfully trusting of you not to secure my other arm. What if I decide to attack you?"

She scoffed and led me down the hall. "I saw the x-rays. You don't have the strength. Plus, I'm sure the pain would be unbearable. How is your arm feeling, by the way?"

I raised my eyebrows and stared at her. Was that genuine concern I heard in her voice? She glanced at me.

"We're not all ogres, you know. You are still a human, and I can care about how another human being feels."

"Yeah, but I'm a prisoner. A bad human."

"Why? Because you helped the people of North Platte overthrow Liet? It was bound to happen. I know the type of people they were sending out there."

I cocked my head to the side, staring at her. "And what type of people were they?"

"Free thinkers, activists. The type of people who might question authority." She shrugged. "Maybe they were good people, maybe they weren't. It's not my place to judge."

We stepped into the sally port where the van waited. I had a hard time believing what I heard. Private Lamb Chop sounded intelligent, she seemed to understand how the system worked, so why was she content with the situation? Didn't she want more?

I took a seat, and she fastened my seatbelt before climbing into the driver's seat. I stared at the back of her head. Was she an ally? Could I convince her to fight on our side? She looked at me through the rearview.

"I don't know what happened in North Platte, so I have no reason to question why you did what you did. All I know is it scared a lot of people down here. The Families especially. Like I said, it was to be expected."

Death To The Undead

I grunted and averted my gaze out the window. If I said anything, I could incriminate myself. Maybe that's what she was trying to do, get me to talk, tell her what happened, then she'd take it to Liet. Well, I didn't want to play.

The garage door lifted and sun streamed into my window. I squinted at the brightness. The vehicle moved forward. As much as I wanted to believe the private could come to our side, I highly doubted she would. She was a guard, she was afforded more freedom than most. She was the elite, the pampered. More than likely, she was content in her position. Plus, recently, I'd had back luck with people I thought I could trust. You get a little nervous when people try to kill you.

We pulled in front of the high school, and the private hooked me up with the cuffs. We still drew a crowd of onlookers, though this wasn't as large as the last. I chuckled inwardly.

We rode the elevator to the suite. It was like déjà vu as we stepped out the door and into the hall. The bodyguard opened the door for us, the same smirk on his face. I rolled my eyes. How irritating would it be to do the same thing day after day? He opened his mouth to speak, but I interrupted him.

"Your sarcasm and wit are completely wasted on me. You should really use it on someone who appreciates it."

His eyes narrowed to slits. It was childish, but I stuck my tongue out at him as I walked by.

We went to Mrs. Johnson's living room, where she waited for us on the couch. A cup of coffee was in her hand, a look of disappointment on her face. We sat across from her.

She clicked her tongue and set her mug on the coffee table. "You were such a good girl, Krista. You had a few issues with authority, but you still did your job. You could've gone far in Florida."

I snorted. "Yeah, head housekeeper was exactly what I was striving for."

"It would have been a better title than traitor." Her tone was sharp.

The anger threatened to boil out of me. All of my muscles tightened, and my jaw clenched. It took every ounce of self control to keep from screaming at her.

"When did you start caring about what happened in North Platte?"

Mrs. Johnson waved her hand dismissively through the air. "If it affects the people of Florida, it affects me."

"You mean if it threatens your power, then you'll do something about it."

Mrs. Johnson crossed her legs and lifted her mug. She took a sip. Laying her left hand on her lap, she stared into her drink with the other.

"I have a commitment, Krista. I have to protect these people. No one else can or will."

"You don't think they are capable of taking care of themselves?"

"No," she said tersely. "They aren't. Without proper leadership, the world will devolve into anarchy and we'll be no better than the undead creatures that threw us into these dark times."

"Human life would find a way. We're not idiots."

She set her mug back on the table and folded both her arms in her lap. "You have such faith in your fellow man. Do you know who I was before this?"

I sat silently, waiting for her to reply. I did have faith in my fellow humans, surprisingly. After everything I'd been through, I would have assumed I hated them. Yeah, there were a few bad eggs, there always were, but for the most part, people were good. Even after having several people attempt to kill me, I still believed humanity was worth saving.

"I was the wife of the Secretary of Defense. I was there the day the zombies first rose."

I listened as she began telling her story.

***

Mrs. Johnson stood next to her husband's desk, waiting patiently so they could go to lunch. He talked on the phone, frowning.

"Have the reports been confirmed?" He listened to the voice on the other end. He ran his hand through his hair and sighed. "Call an emergency meeting. This needs to be taken care of." He hung up and buried his face in his hands.

"Everything all right, dear?" Mrs. Johnson's stomach tightened, her fingers tingled with nervousness.

Mr. Johnson looked up. "Remember those experiments I told you the terrorists were conducting?"

She placed a hand on her chest. "The biological ones?"

He nodded grimly. "It seems they have achieved some results."

Mrs. Johnson sucked in a sharp breath. It couldn't be. It was just a scare tactic. They were trying to force the U.S.'s hand. They weren't actually going to use biological weapons. That would be catastrophic. It was against the rules of war.

"Are you sure?"

Mr. Johnson stood and grabbed her hand. "The source is reliable, and they have some video evidence. Come to the meeting with me. See for yourself."

Mrs. Johnson clicked her tongue. "You know I can't do that. It's against policy."

"I make the policy! I've been receiving reports for months now about what these people have been trying to accomplish. It seemed so far fetched as to be unbelievable. If they've really accomplished their goal, the world will never be the same." He sighed and lowered his voice. "I need you there. Please. No one will even notice you." He grabbed a yellow legal pad and pen off his desk, thrusting them at her. "Here, take notes for me. You can be my assistant. No one will question you being my assistant."

Death To The Undead

Mrs. Johnson had never seen her husband so worried. His face lost color, his eyes were wide. Beads of sweat formed on his forehead. How could she deny him?

She grabbed the paper and pen from him. "All right. I'll go to your meeting."

The conference room hummed with indistinguishable conversations as everyone speculated in groups about what was going on. All eyes turned to Mr. Johnson as he walked to his chair. Mrs. Johnson took a seat at the back of the room, trying to remain inconspicuous.

Mr. Johnson didn't sit. He placed his fists on the table and leaned forward. Worry pinched his face, he looked nauseous.

"Our greatest fears have come to fruition. The one scenario we never thought could happen has happened. General Scorvid, your report please."

All eyes focused on the General. The lights in the room clicked off, and the big screen TV sprang to life.

"This video just came to us this morning. We still don't know how they manufactured the virus, or if it is even a virus, but we do know it works."

The picture shook, focused on a concrete floor, then flipped upward and settled on a row of fluorescent lights. Disembodied voices sounded off camera, speaking in a language Mrs. Johnson couldn't place.

" 'Blue Phoenix test twenty-four,' " someone in the room translated. " 'After several changes to earlier formulas, we believe we have found the right mixture. Push that button. The one on the side.' They're trying to figure the camera out," the translator explained.

Whoever held the camera righted it, focusing on what appeared to be a dead American soldier. He was dressed in green army fatigues, blood soaked through the tank top on his chest. His blonde hair was cut in a spike, his eyes stared blankly at the ceiling.

A man in surgical scrubs stepped into the field of view from the right. His face was covered with a mask, sunglasses covered his eyes. He was intent on being completely anonymous. He approached the body. He held a needle up for everyone to see. Dark blue liquid filled the syringe. He jabbed the needle into the soldier's neck and pumped the fluid in before quickly stepping away from the body.

The camera jostled again, and the sounds of scuffling feet filled the room. Something clanked, and briefly, the links of a chain link fence appeared on the screen. The man with the camera moved so the lens was between the links, giving a clear view of the body.

Minutes passed. Nothing happened. The room sat in stunned silence. In the darkness, Mrs. Johnson saw a few heads turn to their neighbors. She sensed that people wanted to ask what was going on, but no one said a word. A small thud sounded from the TV, and all eyes focused back on the screen.

Death To The Undead

The soldier's hand twitched, thumping on the table. Then, the foot moved. More foreign whispers sounded off camera.

" 'The serum targets the primal parts of the brain, the ones that control simple motor function and basic survival needs. They don't actually need food, their other systems don't work, but the mind thinks they do. They'll attack others, believing humans are an easy source of nourishment.' "

The soldier sat up. The tension in the meeting room grew. The body on the table turned toward the camera. His face was badly burned, half of it charred black, the left eyelid completely missing. It moaned, a low, rumbling sound that could have come from Hell itself. It moved toward the fence, falling face first off the table.

Mrs. Johnson panted. She brought her hand back up to her chest, her heart beat rapidly under her palm. She wanted to turn away, close her eyes from the horror, but she couldn't, she had to know what happened next.

The soldier got to his feet and slowly limped toward the camera, his hand outstretched, his jaw opened and closed, anticipating a bite. The men behind the fence stepped back as the creature slammed into the metal. It reached for them, unable to navigate the links. Another moan sounded, even more disturbing than the last. Chills ran through Mrs. Johnson's body.

The voices spoke again.

" 'Determination for basic necessity make the creature unstoppable. It runs purely on instinct. Any shred of human emotion and reasoning has been eradicated. The only way to stop it is by ceasing the limited functions of the brain.' "

The doctor appeared once again on the screen, a large black Desert Eagle in his hand. He raised the barrel to the soldier's head and pulled the trigger. Even on camera, the bang was deafening. Mrs. Johnson jumped. Blood splattered the lens, and the creature crumpled to the ground. The screen went black.

The lights clicked back on, illuminating the pale faces of the crowd. No one spoke; they barely looked at one another. What had they just seen? Was it real? Did they really witness a dead body being brought back to life? It had to be some sort of trick, a hoax. It had to be.

"We know two things from this video," Mr. Johnson finally broke the silence, though his voice was barely over a whisper. "We know they have figured out how to bring the dead back to life, and we know how to kill them. A shot to the head seems to take them down." He finally sat in his seat. "We weren't meant to get this video. The terrorists were sending it to their Generals, and our ground troops intercepted it. Several brave men and women lost their lives getting this to us. We have the knowledge, now we must do something with it."

"What?" It was the President. His hand was over his stomach, and he burped. He attempted to keep the vomit down. "We don't even know what they're planning on doing."

"And we shouldn't give them the chance to do it," General Scorvid chimed in. "We have to act, and act now. If this thing gets out, it could devastate the country. The world."

"I can't authorize any action based on this video. We can't tell the people of America that our greatest enemies have figured out how to raise the dead. First of all, they wouldn't believe us. Secondly, the panic it would cause would be monumental."

"Then send in a covert operation. Take this threat out before it gets out of hand," General Scorvid said.

The President sat silently, staring at the desk and contemplating. He looked up, his mouth pressed in a tight line. "Do what you have to. But keep it quiet. No one finds out how this started."

***

"Two days later," Mrs. Johnson fought back the tears, "the attacks happened on a global scale. We were too late. By the time we got the video, syringes of the stuff were on their way to every capital in every country. The armed forces did what they were told to do, and they kept things quiet. Unfortunately, they couldn't save everyone." She took a sip of her coffee. "We set up bases, secret places to study the zombies, hoping to find a cure, but the creatures never made it. The disease spread too fast."

"So fix it now," I snapped. "Figure out if it's actually a disease or just wipe the menace off the face of the earth."

"It's too late." She pressed her lips into a thin line. "The damage has been done. The only thing we can do now is survive."

"Is that what your husband would've wanted?"

"He would've wanted to know I was safe and I did my best to protect others." She stood from the couch and glanced out the window.

If I had the chance, I would have attacked her and pushed her through the glass. Lucky for her, I was chained up.

"What happened to your husband?"

She took a deep breath. "He was killed following the President's orders and protecting the American people. He was a true hero."

Death To The Undead

CHAPTER 16

"You hag!"

I couldn't keep my disdain and contempt in check any longer. If I could stand and point an accusatory finger at her, I would've, but my only free hand was cuffed to another person. I squeezed the couch cushion.

"You knew what was going on, and you did nothing to prepare the people?"

She turned, her eyes wide, and opened her mouth to speak. I refused to let her say another word.

"Even if you didn't tell them it was zombies, you still could've told them something. It was a biological attack, let them know. Give them a chance to protect themselves, to prepare. Instead, you let them get killed!" Spit flew out of my mouth, my face burned with rage. "Now, you're trying to make up for it? Now you're trying to keep them safe?" I huffed and snorted. "If you want to make a difference, take some of those helicopters and shoot the undead from the sky. Don't use it to kill innocent people who only wanted a better life. Get rid of the infestation! Capture a few and study them, see if there's a cure. Don't keep people trapped in Florida. It's no longer about feeling guilty, it's about power and control!"

Her eyes narrowed, she pushed her mouth into a thin line. "I made a promise to my husband and the country. I'll see that through."

"Promise? What promise? To keep the people in the dark and as slaves? The only person you're helping by doing that is yourself!"

She walked to the back of the couch, her bony hands clenched in tight fists. "I didn't bring you here to have you mock me. I wanted to give you some insight into what we're dealing with and the impossibility of destroying it. I wanted you to see the difficult situation I'm in, and how your act of rebellion threatens every fiber of our existence."

Who did this woman think she was? Did she really just make the whole zompocalypse about her? Did she place herself as the center of the universe? My body shook with anger. I wanted nothing more than to lash out at her, grab her around the throat and bash her head into the floor until she realized how selfish she was being, but I couldn't. Instead, I lowered my voice and spoke between gritted teeth.

"The only threat to our existence is the undead menace roaming the west and you and The Families who refuse to do anything about it. You can't hide in Florida forever." I sprung to my feet and jerked on the handcuff. "Take me back to jail. I can't listen to another word this woman has to say."

Private Lamb Chop slowly got to her feet, glancing from me to Mrs. Johnson, her eyes wondering what she should do. Mrs. Johnson nodded, and we headed for the door.

I sat in the van, wringing my hand against my pant leg. How could they have not acted? They knew the threat in front of them, why didn't they do more? Why didn't they try harder to stop it? Or warn the people? They had two days. Well, technically, they probably had longer, but they refused to believe what was going on. Those jerkwads! They doomed us!

Maybe not everyone would have been saved, but it would have been a lot more than doing nothing! It was unfathomable, unbelievable that they wouldn't give us a chance. People could be panicky and fall into mob mentality, but there were ways to ensure it didn't happen. Give the people some facts, some information, and a way to combat the threat. It's when the masses don't know what's going on that they believe lies and fall prey to suggestion.

If anyone had the right to believe the human race was full of idiots, it was me. How many people had tried to kill me since the dead rose from their graves? Plus, I used to study serial killers, I knew how evil humans could be. But I didn't believe for one second that the race was incapable of taking care of itself. Yeah, there would always be those individuals out there who would try to take advantage of others. They would see the lawless times as their opportunity to take what they wanted. The Families and Liet were a perfect example. But they could be taken care of. The people needed a leader, for sure, but one who could see what was best for everyone, or at least the vast majority. They needed one who would take action against the undead, not cower in Florida and hope it would eventually go away.

"You doing all right back there?" Private Lamb Chop glanced at me through the rearview.

"Peachy," I growled.

"You know, not to defend them or anything, but at the time, they probably thought they were doing what was best for the country."

"Fine. We can't change what they did to lead to our demise. But The Families have choices. They have helicopters and fire power. Do you know how easy it would be to take out the zombies from the air? They need to do something."

"They are happy here. And so are most of the people. You didn't have to go into the West."

Why did people keep saying that? Yes, I had a choice, and I made it. I didn't want to stay in Florida. Would my life have been easy? Probably. But there's more to living than just existing. If I had to do it all over again, I would make the same decisions I already made.

"It's our country," I spoke between gritted teeth. "Why would we let them win? Why should we hide while the zombies roam free? We can take it back. We should." I focused my gaze out the window.

Why was I wasting my breath? She didn't care. I had to get out of jail. I had to get Bill and Kyle free. If Florida didn't want our help, fine, they wouldn't get it. But I refused to die down here. If I was going to be killed, it was going to be on my terms. Not because some ninny thought I went against her stupid rules.

Death To The Undead

The rest of the drive was accomplished in silence, as was the walk back to my cell. I kept my back to Private Lamb Chop until I heard the door click shut behind me. I hurried to the bars.

"What's going on?" Bill asked.

"We've got to get out of here," I told him.

Kyle folded his arms across his chest. "That's a wonderful plan. How do you expect to accomplish it?"

"Quinn showed me that every jail has a fake block in the ceiling. Like the hatch by the guard desk, it's a means of getting people into the jail to stop a riot."

"Yeah? So? It's in the hall. How are we supposed to get into the hall if we're locked in our cells?"

Bill's attitude irritated me. Wasn't he the one who said I needed to figure something out? Why was he crapping on all my ideas? I took a deep breath and attempted to calm down.

"Do you mind working with me a little? I haven't thought that far. I was hoping you two could help me. Sheesh!"

Bill held up his hands in surrender. "I'm sorry. You're right. Give us a minute. We'll see what we can come up with."

"Thank you." I was about to head to my cot when the door opened and stopped me.

Private Lamb Chop stepped into the hallway, followed by Pearl. My mouth dropped open.

"You have a visitor." She turned to Pearl. "Make it quick. I can only keep the cameras off for a few minutes."

Pearl nodded and stepped into the room. She walked up to my cell and placed her hands on the bars.

"Hey, how are you doing?"

I blinked, wondering if she was actually there or if I fell asleep.

"Look, I don't have much time." She shifted her weight from one foot to the other. "But I might have a way to get you out of here."

"Why would you do that?"

She cocked her head to the side, hurt covering her face. "You're my friend. You don't deserve this."

There was a soft knock on the door.

"I have to go. Be ready for the power outage."

She hurried down the hall and out the door. I stared at Bill and Kyle.

Kyle shook his head. "It's a good thing you have friends down here."

"I guess. Pearl is the last person I would expect to help us. And who knows what the private is planning. Stay on your guard."

***

We spent the rest of the day hanging out in our cells, waiting. I paced the tiny space, chewing on my nails, trying to figure out what was going on. Pearl wasn't one for action. Never had been. She was afraid to leave Florida, scared to death of zombies. Why would she go out of her way to help us now?

And that private. Man, I had no idea what to think about her. She talked the talk, sounded like she wanted to change the world, but was she serious? I didn't know her, I couldn't trust her. Then, she made it a point to tell me Liet asked her to stay on and watch me. That really didn't instill me with confidence. Liet, as creepy and ugly as he was, had a way with women. It must have been the power thing because he could convince them to do strange things for him. And I'm not talking about gross sexual things. Remember the girl who attacked me in his office? Those kinds of things. What if he convinced Private Lamb Chop to let me out and turn me over to him so he could kill me? He had several chances, but he never took them. Something was seriously wrong with that man, but I wouldn't put it past him to eventually take his revenge. Never trust the insane.

Dinner came and went. Nothing. When the guard came in and told us it was lights out, I began to wonder if anything was going to happen at all. Pearl wasn't exactly specific of when to expect anything. She just said to be ready. For all I knew, she could have meant in two days.

I laid on my cot and stared at the ceiling. Maybe it was too much for me to get my hopes up. Maybe Private Lamb Chop told Mrs. Johnson about Pearl's visit and Pearl was in custody. Maybe she was dead. Maybe she changed her mind. Either way, I needed to figure out how to get us out.

I was drifting to sleep when a loud clunk echoed through the hallway. It wasn't a something-was-dropped clunk, but one of those sounds you hear right before the power goes out. Like a circuit breaker clicking off. Of course, it was hard to tell since the lights were off for night time anyway. I looked at the door for a while, waiting for something else to happen. Maybe shouts coming from the other side of the door, or moans sounding from zombies. But there was nothing. There wouldn't be zombies, we were in Florida, but I did expect some type of ruckus. Still, it was too weird. I got up and headed to the door. Curiously, I placed my hands on the bars and pushed. To my amazement, the door slid open. I had to be dreaming. I glanced into the hallway. Bright white emergency lights illuminated the floor. I stepped across the hall to Bill's cell. He laid on his cot, his back to me. I pushed open his door. He turned and looked at me over his shoulder.

"What's going on?"

"I don't know," I whispered. "But let's not question it." I moved to Kyle's cell.

He was already at his door, pushing it to the side.

The three of us proceeded with caution to the main door. I glanced through the small window. The corner of the guard's desk was barely visible. Nothing moved. Silently, I turned the handle and peered through the crack. Private Lamb Chop stood behind the desk, her arms folded over her chest. She smiled at me.

"We haven't got all day," she said quietly. "The night shift will be here any minute."

My stomach tingled. My first inclination was to head back into my cell, crawl into bed, and pretend like nothing ever happened. It all seemed too convenient. Too easy. We were walking into a trap, we had to be. Lately, things hadn't been going my way. I was about to turn around, too, but Bill and Kyle pushed me through the door. Private Lamb Chop hurried us to the sally port and into the van. We drove through the streets to Tanya's storage yard.

"Head to row Q," the private instructed. "Shed eight will be unlocked."

Without asking any questions, we climbed out of the van and looked for row Q. The vehicle drove off, and I stared after it for a long time. Any minute, she was going to turn back around and climb out, laughing. She'd have a gun in her hand and tell us it was all a joke. The taillights disappeared on the horizon.

We found shed 8 and lifted the door. It was empty, except for a bare light bulb that barely illuminated the room.

"What now?" Kyle asked.

I shrugged. "I say we make a break for it. Why are we hanging out in a shed waiting to be captured? No one knows we're gone, we can hot wire a car and head for the border."

"You don't want to do that," a familiar voice spoke behind us.

We turned to the door. Pearl ducked under it, hidden mostly in shadows.

"And why not?" My defenses went up. If she was planning on doing something treacherous, I wanted to be ready.

"Because then you won't be able to take down The Families."

I glanced from her to the brothers. How did she know what we planned? And why was she willing to help us?

She stepped up to me and embraced me in a hug. It felt good to be in her arms, but she squeezed a little too tight, causing pain to burn through my shoulder. I let out an involuntary squeak. She pulled away.

"Sorry," she said as she wiped tears away from her eyes. "And I'm sorry I didn't help you sooner. I had no idea what Mrs. Johnson and the others were doing. I heard the story she told you earlier today, and I heard what happened in North Platte. Liet is one angry individual."

I still felt like I was in a dream. I willed myself to fly, even making slight hops to see if I could get airborne. Pearl stared at me in confusion.

"Are you all right?"

I shook my head. "I don't know. I think I might be dreaming."

"You're not dreaming," Pearl assured me. "This is very real." She hugged me again. "When I saw you chained up to Mark, I couldn't believe it. I thought for sure someone had made a mistake. Then, I heard Liet telling Mrs. Johnson about the rebellion. I remembered our conversation on the balcony the last time you were here, and how much of a rebel you actually are, and put two and two together. I couldn't let you die for doing what you believed was right."

"Who's Mark?" I knew it wasn't the most important question I could've asked at that particular moment, but it seemed like the only one that mattered.

"Mrs. Johnson's bodyguard."

"Ah. How did you get the private to help you out?"

"Abby has been a friend for a long time."

"I thought you didn't want to get involved in this sort of thing."

The wrinkles on her forehead deepened. "What sort of thing are you talking about?"

I gestured with my arm, forming a circle. "This. Aiding and abetting traitors. Helping with the rebellion."

A pained look crossed her face. "Why would you think that?"

"Because the last time I talked to you, you told me you never wanted to leave Florida. You said you were content living the life you were living. You didn't understand how I could live my life right next to the zombies."

"I was afraid, I admit that. And you can't blame me. There's a lot out there that I don't know. But I can't let justice and what is right be trampled on. Especially when it comes to my best friend." A small smile crawled across her lips. "Besides, my uncle is sympathetic to your cause. He wants to help. He's not the only one. There are others who share your vision of taking back our country."

Bill and Kyle stepped forward.

"How many?" Bill asked.

"Well, not as many as there had been. A lot of them were sent to North Platte, but there's still enough to launch a formidable attack."

"Do you have a plan?" Kyle inquired.

The smile on her lips grew wider. "We do. And now that you're free, you can help."

Death To The Undead

CHAPTER 17

I needed time to figure things out, to ask questions, but I wasn't going to get it. We had a small window of opportunity, and we needed to act. We were already branded as traitors, it wasn't going to be long before they discovered we'd escaped, too. Then, everyone in Florida would hunt us. I had to set my doubts and suspicions aside. Even if I died trying to free the people from tyranny, at least it wouldn't be in vain. And if Abby or Pearl tried to take me down, I'd make sure I didn't go down alone.

"So, where are they?" Pearl asked.

"Where are what?"

"The weapons. When Tanya came into Mrs. Johnson's apartment and told her about Bill and Kyle, she said she stashed some weapons for the rebellion."

"Well, I would assume Mrs. Johnson confiscated those weapons for her personal use."

Pearl shook her head. "No. She told Mark to leave them where they're at. A secret stash in case they need them later."

My, that was awfully convenient. Who knows what she planned on doing with them. I wouldn't put anything past that woman.

"I have no idea where Tanya kept them. I left and never planned on coming back. Did she tell Mrs. Johnson where they were?"

Pearl's shoulders slumped forward. "No. Tanya said she'd tell her when she came back. How are we going to find them?"

Not a bad plan on Tanya's part. Insurance that nothing happened to her once she came back with me. And if something happened to her, they'd have to tear the place apart to find them. Perhaps raising suspicions. Maybe she wasn't an idiot after all.

"Maybe she kept records in her coffee shop," Kyle suggested.

Pearl brightened slightly. "Maybe. We should check it out."

"Is it really that good of an idea to be traipsing around this town looking for guns?" I asked. "I mean, once they figure out we're gone, it's the first place they are going to send the soldiers. Mrs. Johnson knows about them, so she'll assume that's where we're going. We need to be unpredictable."

"How does she know where to send them if she doesn't know where they are?" Pearl wondered.

The three of them stared at me.

"Good question. I don't know." Oh, yeah. We did have an advantage. Still, it seemed risky.

"Okay," Bill said. "What do you suggest?"

I shrugged. "I don't really know. I just know we need to figure something else out. First and foremost, we need to find a place to hide. Preferably outside of city limits."

They all nodded.

"There's some cars in storage over there," Kyle pointed to his right. "We could hotwire one of them and head out."

"Good. Let's do it."

We stepped out of the storage shed and pulled the door down as quietly as we could. Keeping an eye on our surroundings, we hurried across the storage yard. It took slightly longer than we expected, but we got an old Cadillac running. On our way out of town, we drove past the high school. I glanced at it with disdain. We were going to take them down. Even if we had to burn all of Florida to the ground. Someone stepped out the front door as we drove by. If I didn't know any better, I would have sworn it was Tanya. I spun in my seat to get a better view, but she was out of sight. I turned to the others.

"Did you see that?"

Kyle looked out the back window, and Pearl stared at me.

"See what?" Bill looked through the rearview.

"I swear I just saw Tanya."

They stared at me, confusion covering their faces.

"But it couldn't be," Pearl said. "Isn't she still out west?"

I tried to do the calculations in my head. How long would it have taken her to get here? If they left right after Liet and I did, she could have made it hours after we did. But why would she come down here? She failed at her mission. She didn't bring me back. Besides, she had nothing to offer The Families. Liet knew where the others hid, he could lead the army there himself. Maybe having me captured was good enough. Maybe she could still come back and live in comfort. I couldn't worry about it. We had other things to do.

"Hey," I looked at Pearl. "What happened to Liet?"

I couldn't allow him to continue to run free. He was a threat to us, no matter what. If we were going to take Florida down, Liet had to go with it. And this time, he wasn't going to get away with his life.

"He was going to shower and rest. That's all I know. Mrs. Johnson set him up in a suite at the high school. She also told Mark to have someone keep an eye on him. She was afraid he'd try to hurt you."

"We need to know where he's at."

Kyle stared at me. "You can't make this a personal mission."

"I'm not. Liet has to be taken care of. If anything is going to mess up our chances at taking out The Families, it's him. He knows what we're capable of, and he knows how to fight against it. Once he finds out we're missing, he'll do everything in his power to hunt us down."

Kyle looked at Bill, who sighed. "What do you want to do?"

"We need to neutralize him."

"And we can," Pearl chimed in, "but now is not the time. My uncle had a plan. Once we get out of town, I'll contact him. He'll meet us and let us know what's going on."

I pursed my lips. "Why didn't you mention that while we were at the shed?"

"I wasn't supposed to contact him until I had the weapons. There was less risk of being found out. But since we can't get the guns, we have to figure something else out."

I balled my hand into a fist. Why did everything have to be so difficult? Why couldn't things work out for us like they did in North Platte? In reality, why were we even wasting our time? We could easily take the vehicle back to the West and disappear. No one would find us, and we could live out our lives in relative peace. It would be a lonely existence, especially without Quinn, but we'd be alive.

"Stop the car!" I shouted.

Bill swerved, startled by my outburst. "What?"

"I said stop the car. If Tanya was back there, we can get the weapons. We don't have to reformulate a plan."

He pulled over onto the side of the road and stared at me in disbelief. "Do you really think walking back to the high school is such a good idea? They'll find you, you'll get recaptured."

I shook my head. "They won't get me again. I won't allow it. I'll go back and see if it was Tanya, you guys contact Pearl's uncle. If all goes well, we'll meet back at the storage yard at six in the morning."

"And what if it doesn't go well?" Bill's tone bordered on furious.

"Then I'll see you back in jail."

I didn't wait for an answer; I opened the door and jumped out of the car. I hurried behind a building and got out of sight. I pressed my back against the wall and waited until I couldn't hear the car anymore. How was I going to get back to the high school? There were so many lights! If I were in the West, it wouldn't have been an issue. I glanced down. Crap! I was still wearing my bright orange jumpsuit! Yeah, that wouldn't be a dead give away at all! I needed to find something to cover up with, and quick.

I side-stepped to the end of the building and glanced around the corner. Streetlights illuminated the sidewalk, and a few people milled around. There was a park directly across from me. It was still bright, but there were at least trees to keep me hidden. I waited until the couple closest to me stepped onto the grass before dashing toward a clump of trees. I placed my hand on the trunk and got my bearings. The high school was three blocks in front of me. Lights shone on the building, lighting it up like a Christmas tree. I doubted Tanya was still there. If that was her I saw, she walked out of the building, which meant she probably headed back to her apartment above the coffee shop. Still, it was three blocks I had to go. Why weren't people in their homes?

It's not any different than alluding a zombie, I told myself. In fact, it's easier. Most people probably wouldn't give me a second glance. Once they noticed the jail attire, they'd go find help instead of taking me on. A zombie would hunt me relentlessly. I could do it. I had to do it.

Death To The Undead

Still, the least amount of attention I could draw to myself, the better. I headed off through the trees.

It took me a while, but I made it to the back of the coffee shop. I crouched in the alley, next to a dumpster, and stared at the second story window. Soft orange light drifted from the glass, and a shadow moved on the ceiling. Someone was in there. I could only hope it was Tanya. There was a fire escape. Perfect. I snuck over to it and grabbed the bottom step. I glanced around before placing my feet onto the ladder. Using my elbow strapped in the sling, I secured myself to the rungs. Pain rippled through my shoulder, but I tolerated it to get to my goal. With a bit of effort and some grunting, I made it to the top landing. I pressed my back against the wall and peeked into the room.

The window looked onto a small square kitchen table with white laminate covering. Four white wooden chairs with slatted backs were pushed up on each side of the table. A basket of plastic-looking fruit sat in the center. Beyond the dining room was a couch and TV, which wasn't on. The living room was dark. There must have been hallways on either side of the living room that led to bedrooms, but I couldn't see them. Nothing moved. If Tanya was in there, she wasn't in the dining room or living room. I risked a deeper glance. To the left of the dining room was the kitchen, as dark as the living room.

I moved back against the wall and took a deep breath. Crouching down, I positioned myself under the window. I mentally crossed my fingers, hoping the window was unlocked. I pushed up against the frame. The window slid open. *Thank you*! I pushed it open further, keeping an eye on the room beyond. Still, nothing moved.

When I had a space big enough to crawl through, I delicately placed my leg inside. The floor wasn't far, and I set my foot down gently. Nothing. I ducked my body under and paused, listening. The only sound was my heart beating in my chest. I worked my entire body through the window. I quickly skittered into the kitchen, hiding in the cover of darkness. I kept my breathing calm and under control as I surveyed the area.

I found what I looked for: a knife block. I grabbed a steak knife. Normally, people would grab a butcher knife or some other big knife, but that's not always the best weapon. It's big and clunky, which means it can be easily knocked out of your hand. With one of my arms out of commission, I needed something small I could easily keep a grip on. A small knife against the neck would inflict just as much damage as a large one, especially if you get the right spot. With the knife firmly in my hand, the back of the blade comfortable against my forearm, I headed toward the living room.

That's another thing you see people doing wrong. You don't want the blade directly out in front of you. It's reflective, which means it will shine light into your target's eyes, giving away your position. Plus, if they see the blade first, they can knock it out of your hand. If you hold it against your arm, you have a lot more chances of actually sneaking up on your opponent and keeping hold of your weapon. Plus, if they attacked you, you could inflict damage by blocking. Pam taught me that in North Platte. It was part of my training to prepare me for the zombie-infested West. Of course, zombies wouldn't recognize a knife or realize the threat, but it was still a good skill to have.

I paused when I reached the edge of the living room and glanced to both sides. As I suspected, hallways led to other rooms. But which one was Tanya's? Suddenly, a thought occurred to me. What if I just snuck into the wrong house? What if there was more than one apartment above the coffee shop? One scream from an elderly lady and the jig was up.

Stop that! I told myself. *You're in the right spot. Focus.*

A soft shuffling sounded to my right. My head jerked in that direction. On my tiptoes, I made my way down the hall. I stopped at the door and pressed my ear to the wood. The shuffling sounded again. Closer, it sounded like feet moving under sheets. I tucked the knife into my sling and reached for the handle. With painfully slow movements, I turned the handle and opened the door. Like the other parts of the house, the room was dark. Someone lay on the bed on their left side. I pulled the knife back out of the sling. Biting my lower lip, I stepped into the room. I moved toward the side of the bed where their back was. I held my breath.

I reached the edge of the bed and peered down. The hair was blonde, the build looked like Tanya. I flipped the knife around so the blade was out.

"Pssst," I said softly.

The body moved, rolling onto her back. The gray light from the window above the bed illuminated her face. Her eyes were open, brow furrowed in confusion. It was Tanya. She screamed when she noticed me and tried to scramble away. I sat on the bed, on her legs. I wasn't worried about anyone hearing. I figured she was alone in the apartment, and the closest neighbors were across the street.

"I wouldn't do that if I were you," I whispered.

She clicked on the light next to her bed. Her eyes were wide, wild. Recognition sparked, and she visibly relaxed.

"Oh, my God, Krista! You scared the hell out of me!"

Footsteps sounded in the hall. Running footsteps. I slid up her legs so I was on her thighs, placing the knife against her neck. I didn't have another hand, and I didn't want to risk Tanya getting away. I hated my back being toward the door, but I didn't have another choice. I glanced over my shoulder.

At first, the only thing I saw was a gun, the barrel pointed directly at me. I pressed the knife into Tanya's flesh. She squeaked.

"Krista?" The voice was familiar.

"Pam?"

Pam lowered her gun.

"What are you doing here?" Confusion crept through my body.

Someone moved behind her. I averted my gaze to the new person. The knife dropped from my hand, my breath caught in my throat.

"Quinn?" I barely got the name out of my throat.

He smiled and stepped into the room.

I was afraid to move. I thought if I stood up, I would actually wake up and he would fade into mist. He walked to the side of the bed and placed his hand on my cheek. It was warm. The calluses scratched my skin. I closed my eyes briefly and reopened them. He was still there. I sprung to my feet and wrapped my good arm around his neck. Tears flowed freely from my eyes. I pulled back and touched his face with my fingertips, tracing his eyebrow, down his cheek, and across his lips. He leaned forward and kissed me. I wrapped my arm around his neck once again, pulling him tight. I didn't want to let him go.

"I thought you died," I whispered.

"I would have if it weren't for you."

I pulled back and looked into his eyes.

"Liet shot me, there's no denying that. But when you bumped him, the shot hit my midsection." He stepped back and lifted his shirt. A white bandage circled his stomach. "Thankfully, it was the meaty part. Missed my vital organs. I think it was a twenty-two. Anything larger would have torn me up. Still hurt like hell, though."

"We dragged him out of the cave as soon as you and Liet disappeared into the trees," Pam explained. "We tried to convince Quinn to stay behind, to heal up, but he refused. We warned the people at camp about what happened and took a truck. We figured he'd bring you down here. We had to fix Quinn in the car."

"It was a nasty patch job," Tanya interjected, "but we stopped the bleeding."

"We found some pharmacies along the way and got me some antibiotics. I'll have a scar, but I'm no worse for the wear." Quinn smiled at me.

"How did you get past the border guards?" I asked.

"That's where I came in." Tanya stood from the bed, placing the knife on the night stand. "I was sent out to capture you, remember? The guards at the gate knew to expect me, and those two hid in the back of the truck. We drove right in."

I glanced from her to Quinn, eyes wide. He wasn't supposed to know. He placed a hand on my shoulder.

"It's okay." He nodded, as if the action would reassure me. "She confessed to me on the way down. She had to. We wouldn't have gotten in otherwise." He stared at her. "I almost left her on the side of the road." Anger burned in his pupils, but I knew he didn't have another choice. He focused back on me. "We're here now. We're going to make everything all right." He chuckled. "Of course, we did think we were going to have to rescue you. This kind of changes our plans."

I hugged him again. I still had trouble believing he was in front of me.

"What are you doing here anyway?" Pam questioned.

"After Pearl helped us escape, we were driving by and I noticed Tanya at the high school." I focused on Tanya. "What were you doing there anyway?"

"Just telling Mrs. Johnson I was back."

"Did you tell her about the guns?"

She shook her head. "No. I told her I was tired and would talk to her about them later. She waved me away, said it didn't matter. She said they had more important concerns to worry about at the moment."

I turned back to Quinn and Pam. "I came here to make her tell me where the weapons are stashed."

"Why?" Pam placed her hands on her hips.

"Because the rebellion is still on. Pearl has people, and they want to help."

The three of them smiled.

"Great!" Quinn exclaimed. "What do we need to do?"

"We're meeting at the storage yard at six."

"Perfect. I brought your weapons. And you need a change of clothes." He kissed the tip of my nose. "Orange is not your color."

CHAPTER 18

Everyone goes through a rough patch, but it doesn't last forever. The best way to get through it is to keep your head up and hope in your heart. I heard Dad saying those words. It usually preceded the Rome comment. I cringed when those words came out of his mouth, wondering if he really knew what he said. How could he possibly understand the depth and importance of the crisis I was going through when he said those things to me? That's when I was young. I thought Dad was crazy, out of touch. In reality, he had an idea. Like most parents, he'd experienced enough to know what he talked about.

As I walked hand in hand with Quinn to the storage yard, I thought of those words. We hit a rough patch, one that almost cost our lives. Things were turning around, though. We might make it out. I wouldn't say things got better because I kept my head up and had hope. Heck no. In fact, I was about ready to give up, call it quits, and succumb to my fate. It was a good thing there were people around me who could lend a helping hand when I needed it most.

I still couldn't believe Quinn was right next to me. I kept staring at him and tightening my grip on his hand, expecting him to vanish at any moment. I suddenly felt very guilty for the thoughts I had when I was in my cell. Thankfully, I didn't have to explain my inner musings to anyone but myself, and they were pretty much a moot point since he was alive. I promised myself I would never let him go again. I promised I would fall in love with him.

The sun crept over the horizon, casting orange and pink hues onto the city. The heat rose, also. The four of us crept across the street into the storage yard, glancing nervously at our surroundings. I wasn't as conspicuous without my orange jumpsuit, but there weren't a lot of escaped traitors running around with their arm in a sling. It wouldn't have been hard to recognize me.

"Where do we meet them?" Tanya whispered.

"Shed Q eight."

She nodded and headed for the row. Again, we glanced around nervously, then lightly knocked on the door. Moments passed. There was no answer.

"Are you sure they're here?" Pam wondered.

I shrugged. "They're supposed to be. Unless something happened to them." My stomach fluttered.

Tanya knocked again, slightly louder.

"Why don't we just lift the door?" Quinn suggested.

"What if they have guns?" I asked.

"It's a risk we'll have to take." He bent down to grab the handle when the door flew upward.

I placed my hand over my gun, suddenly aware we might walk into a trap. Several hours had passed since our escape, and it was safe to assume the entire city was on high alert. With any luck, they thought we left, but Liet knew better. He knew what we wanted to accomplish. We'd have to keep our eyes open.

I relaxed slightly when Bill's thin figure appeared before us. His eyes scanned each of us intently, narrowing when they got to Tanya, but widening when they fell upon Quinn.

"Quinn?" He reached forward and wrapped his arms around his shoulders, drawing him into a hug.

Kyle joined them.

"Krista said you were dead." Bill held Quinn at arm's length.

Kyle looked up, his eyes glistened with tears.

"And I probably would've been if it wasn't for her." He glanced at me. "She bumped Liet just in time." He smiled.

"This reunion is very touching, but I think we should get inside." Pam's voice had a hint of urgency to it.

Bill stepped back, and we proceeded into the shed. He pulled the door closed and we formed a circle in the middle of the floor. Kyle stood in front of Tanya, his hands on his hips.

"What's she doing here?" The contempt was apparent in his tone.

"Helping us," Pam answered.

Bill spit onto the ground, stirring up a tiny cloud of dust. "Did you know she's the reason we were put into jail in the first place? She's the one who turned us in."

I positioned myself so I was between the brothers and Tanya. I hated being there. If anyone deserved to get revenge on Tanya, it was those two. But we needed her. She was the only one who knew where the weapons were.

"We know," I told them. "Tanya confessed everything to Pam and Quinn. They wouldn't have gotten into Florida without her. And now she's going to make it up to everyone." I looked at her, raising my eyebrows in silent question.

She nodded. "I am. I'm going to make it better." Sympathy covered her face. "I'm sorry for what I did," she told the guys. "I wasn't thinking. I was so mad. If I could take it back, I would." Her voice choked with tears.

I glanced at the brothers. I could tell they weren't convinced, but they didn't look like they were going to attack, either. That was good enough for me. "Okay, now that we've got that out of the way."

I turned to Pearl, who stood at the back of the shed with an older man, probably somewhere in his forties. His hair was salt and peppered, his skin tanned and wrinkled from working in the sun. He had on a pair of khakis and a white polo. I glanced at his shoes. Brown loafers. Not exactly my choice of attire for a takeover, but what did I know? Maybe it was comfortable. The clothes I wore I borrowed from Tanya. Someone might have thought a tank top and jeans weren't the best clothes for a takeover, but I was comfortable.

"Krista, this is my uncle, Tom. I told you about him last time you visited."

He nodded in my direction, then nodded at the others. "It's nice to finally meet you all. Pearl's told me a lot about you, Krista. Especially the most recent events." His eyes flashed with mischief. "I think you and I might have a lot in common."

I placed my hand on the butt of my gun. It wasn't a threatening posture, I just didn't have anywhere else to put my appendage.

"How so?" I asked.

"We have the same goal in mind: getting rid of The Families."

The rest of the group stepped up beside me, which could have definitely been construed as a threatening stance. If anyone walked in at that moment, it would look like we were surrounding Pearl and her uncle, preparing to beat them. But Tom didn't seem fazed.

"We have to take back what's ours. We can't continue to live in fear. I've assembled a group of people who feel the same way. We only need some weapons."

I nodded toward Tanya. "That's where she comes in."

"I stashed them in the crawl space under the coffee shop. I figured it was the best place to keep them hidden. How many people are we talking about here?"

"Hundreds," Tom said. "Dispersed throughout the entire state."

Tanya frowned. "I don't think we have enough weapons for that many people."

"We have a few guns," Tom interjected. "And other weapons to get us by. It would be helpful to have more."

"We'll give you all we have," I said. "And if you need more, you'll have to take them off the guards." A thought occurred to me, and I placed my hand on my head. "Oh, wait! Liet! He brought down a stack of AR fifteens from the cave. We could use those."

Pam stepped forward so I was in her line of sight. "Do you know where they are?"

I glanced at Pearl.

"Right after I saw them take you out of the suite in chains, I caught the end conversation between Mrs. Johnson and Liet. He said something about guns, and she said they wouldn't worry about them right now. Eventually, she wanted him to take them to the gate."

"So, where are they?" Pam asked.

"I assume they're still in the back of the Hummer he brought," Pearl stated.

"And where is it?" Kyle inquired.

Pearl smiled. "The parking lot of the high school."

"Perfect," I said. "We get that vehicle, and you'll have more guns."

Tom nodded. "More guns will definitely help, but we'll still be outnumbered. I have a plan to compensate for that, though."

We all moved closer, anxious to hear what he had to say.

"It will be a coordinated attack. Since we don't have the resources to hold one city and then attack another, we'll attack simultaneously. If we take out each Family, the towns will fall."

"Sounds logical," Quinn stated.

"So," Tom continued, "the easiest way to get in and around the security systems is to cut all of the power in the city. My plan is to take over every power station and hold it while a small group takes The Families hostage. Without power, they'll have to give into our demands. People don't want to live without their luxuries."

We were quiet for a moment, absorbing the information.

"Makes sense," Quinn broke the silence. "Hopefully, it will minimize the amount of lives lost. You'll still have to deal with soldiers, though. They won't be happy about you taking over the power supply."

"We know." Tom nodded. "And we're prepared for that. We've been working on this idea for months."

"So, how do you plan on getting into the power buildings?" I wondered.

"Easy." Tom smiled. "I'm head Electrical Engineer."

I smacked the side of my head. "Of course! Pearl told me that the last time I was down here."

"We've already got things set up. We can electrify the fences around the perimeter, and we have a closed circuit communication system. The last thing we needed was more weapons, just in case. Now that we have those, we're ready to go."

"Sounds like a plan. How long will it take to put in place?" Quinn asked.

"Give me a day, just so I can get the weapons to the furthest cities."

"That's feasible," I said. "But we need to get the Hummer for you. Once that's in our possession, you can take it to where it needs to go."

"Won't someone notice it's missing?" Concern laced Pearl's voice.

"Probably." I shrugged. "But by then, hopefully we'll have the plan in full motion."

"So, who's going to get the Hummer?" Pam stared at me.

"No one knows who you are, except Liet, and I doubt he'll be guarding the vehicle. You take Kyle and go after the Hummer. Bill, you and Tanya will go after the other guns. Pearl, Tom, you tell them where they should meet you."

"What are you and Quinn going to do?" Tanya's tone had a hint of suspicion to it.

"We're going to watch your backs. Neither one of us is in any shape to actually do physical labor. The coffee shop and high school are right next to each other. We can take a position on a roof and let you know if there is trouble. Everyone surely knows about the prison break by now, so they'll be overly cautious. Once everything and everyone is in place, we'll take over the Johnson household."

"There's another thing I should tell you," Tom interjected. "Once we leave here, there's no way to contact each other. The power stations can talk, but using walkies or cell phones is too open. We might be tracked. Wait for the signal before making any move. The signal will be the power going off for three seconds, coming back on for ten, then going off indefinitely."

Cell phones? It boggled my mind to think they still had technology down there.

"How will we know if the takeover is a success?" Pam inquired.

"After the teams have gone into their respective Families' houses, they will call this number." He handed me a card with a number on it. "If we don't hear from you within half an hour of the power outage, we'll send reinforcements."

"Wow." Quinn looked around at all of us. "Sounds like you've got all of your bases covered. Glad to know people down here are willing to help." He looked at me. "Makes our job much easier."

"Good luck to everyone," Tom said. "May we be successful."

We all nodded our agreement.

I turned to Pam, Tanya, and the brothers. "Good luck. Stay safe, and be careful. This is what we planned for, we can do it."

We pulled together in a large circle and hugged. I didn't particularly want Tanya in there with us, and I'm sure the brothers could have lived without hugging her, but she was risking her life. She was going to make it better. And if she didn't, I had no doubts in my mind that Bill would make her pay. That's why I sent them together.

When we pulled away, I turned to Pearl and Tom. I held out my hand, and Tom shook it.

"Thank you for all your help." I wanted to say more, to tell him I owed him my life and what he was doing was going to change the course of history, but the words wouldn't come out. I turned to Pearl. She pulled me into a hug.

"I know you're scared," I whispered in her ear, "but things are gonna be all right. Stick close to your uncle, and you'll be fine."

I pulled back and looked into her face. She nodded and sniffed. I thought she might cry, but she kept her emotions in check.

"When this is over," she pointed a finger at me, "you owe me a week of hanging out."

I smiled. "I promise. But, you have to come to Quinn's ranch to do it."

Her face paled. I couldn't help but chuckle.

"I won't let anything happen to you. Don't worry."

"All right crew," Pam's voice was authorial, but not shouting. "We've got a job to do. Let's head out."

We walked to the door and waited while Bill raised it slightly. Kyle got down onto his stomach and looked through the crack. He made a cutting motion at his neck. I sucked in a breath and held it. I could see the shadow of feet moving under the door.

"What do we do?" Pearl whispered.

Tanya pointed to the back. "Head to the shadows. I'll take care of this."

We did as she instructed. When we were as concealed as we could get, she lifted the door as high as her waist and ducked under. She pushed it closed.

"Oh, hey," we heard Tanya's voice through the door. "What are you doing here this early?"

"Looking for escaped prisoners." The voice was distinctly male, but it didn't sound like Liet. More than likely, it was just some guard. "You see anything suspicious?"

There wasn't a response, so I assumed she shook her head.

"What are you doing out here?"

"You know, just checking things out. We've been having some issues with mice, so I wanted to place some traps."

"With the door closed?"

"Don't need other ones getting in. Plus, that sun beating into the shed makes it really hot."

There was a long silence. What was going on? What was the soldier thinking? He believed her, he had to believe her. We were so screwed if he didn't believe her. I tightened my grip on my gun. I wasn't going to let some minor-league guard ruin our plans. I didn't want to have to kill anyone, but I would. Too much was at stake. And I refused to go back to jail.

Death To The Undead

Eventually, the scuff of dirt drifted into the shed. A few minutes later, the door opened. Tanya signaled with her hand for us to move. We hurried out of the darkness. Squinting, I looked to my right and left, trying to figure out which way the guard had gone. He wasn't anywhere in sight, so I figured we were safe. Tanya and Bill headed toward the coffee shop. Pam and Kyle skulked toward the high school. Pearl and Tom disappeared around the corner.

"We should get on top of that building right there," Quinn pointed. "Looks like maybe it's a convenient store or sandwich place. Either way, it's right between the high school and coffee shop. We'll have a great view of both."

I nodded my agreement. It didn't matter if we were ready or not, the plan was in motion.

CHAPTER 19

I had second thoughts about helping out the inhabitants of Florida. I stood in the alley behind the building, staring up at Quinn as he climbed the access ladder to the roof, and wondered why we didn't just leave. I mean, they seemed to have everything under control. Tom said they'd been planning the attack for months, which means they wanted to do it long before we took over North Platte. They didn't need our help, they could handle things just fine without us.

Well, after we got them their guns they could handle things without us. We didn't really need to put ourselves at risk. If we were captured, they'd shoot us on sight. It was risky enough being in "Johnsons' Town," let alone having to spend an entire day there. Where were we going to go? If we really wanted to, we could crawl down from the roof, take a car, and disappear into the West. But Quinn would never do it. He felt obligated to help them out. He was definitely a better person than I was.

He signaled me from the roof, waving his hand for me to come up. With difficulty, I climbed the ladder. At the top, he grabbed me under the armpits and pulled me onto the roof. Man, it was hot up there! I suddenly missed the wind in the West. It would've cooled me off. Our feet crunched on the gravel as we scurried to the other side to keep an eye on things. Sweat already dripped from my forehead. I hoped they hurried up with their missions.

Death To The Undead

To my right, I saw Tanya and Bill heading into the coffee shop. Bill glanced around nervously. I knew he would feel much more comfortable once he had a weapon. I would. I just hoped he used it on those who were actually deserving and not out of spite. Of course, it could be debated that Tanya deserved to be shot, but she also was allowed the benefit of the doubt. In front of us, Pam and Kyle crouched and headed toward the high school parking lot. From my vantage point, I saw the Hummer parked close to the building. Typical of Liet, he was in a handicap parking space. A guard sat on the bumper, but I don't think he was actually guarding the vehicle. He had a cigarette in his mouth and a relaxed attitude. Why would he think anything was going to happen? If he was watching it, he was probably angry about it and didn't give the job his full attention. That would be detrimental to him. Pam and Kyle weren't going to mess around.

Thankfully, the city still slept. A few cars drove on the streets, some people, maybe teachers, coming to work, but nothing we couldn't handle. A few soldiers milled around, too. They drove the roads in Jeeps, but they headed away from the school, more than likely to do a search of the perimeter and outside of town to find us. They had no reason to believe we'd still be in town. Liet might, knowing we wanted to take things over, but he also knew we didn't have the manpower. He didn't know Quinn was still alive, and The Families thought Tanya was on their side. We had surprise on our side. For a while at least.

We got to the edge of the building and crouched down. A three-foot wall gave us great cover. Quinn had his rifle with him, and his revolver on his hip. I had my handgun, too, but it wasn't going to be much help if I had to shoot too far. If it came down to it, we could only hope the shots would be enough to scare any attackers into cover. With any luck, it wouldn't come down to that. I glanced to my right.

Tanya and Bill disappeared into the building. I looked forward. Pam and Kyle were close, two cars away. The soldier sucked on the last of his cigarette, blissfully unaware of what was going on. Pam and Kyle separated, each heading in a different direction. They were going to surround the Hummer. The guard pushed himself away from the bumper and idly paced around. He was a few feet away from the truck. Pam straightened up and tucked her gun into her waist band at the small of her back. She quickly glanced to see where Kyle was before approaching the man.

My palms began to sweat, my mouth went dry. I didn't know exactly what she was doing, but I hoped it worked. The guard didn't know who she was, he couldn't. Besides, she wasn't wanted like we were. Yeah, if Liet saw her he'd shoot her, but Liet wasn't around. This had to work.

The guard stiffened when he noticed her, tightening his grip on his gun, but he didn't raise the barrel in her direction. Their voices were distant, but I caught the gist of their conversation.

"Hey, man," she had her hands out to her sides to show she wasn't a threat. "Can I bum a cigarette off you?"

The man hesitated for moment, eying her suspiciously.

"Hey, if you don't have any, that's fine." She went to turn around.

"No, here." He reached into his shirt pocket.

"Thanks. I appreciate it." She took the stick from him. "Can I borrow your light too? I'd use mine, but it's in my pocket and I don't want to make you nervous."

He pulled it out and lit the cigarette for her.

"Thanks." She took a long drag. "So, what ya doing out here this early?" The smoke billowed out of her mouth.

"Patrol," he responded.

"Ah. Do you want me to move along? Am I bothering you?"

The guard shrugged one shoulder and opened his mouth to speak. He never got the chance. Kyle approached him from behind and smacked the back of his head with the butt of his gun. The man crumpled, but they didn't let him hit the ground. Pam relieved him of his M4 before dragging him to a bush and placing him under it. They quickly scanned the area again before heading to the Hummer.

Pam approached the driver's side door and placed her hand on the handle. It was going to be locked, I knew it. Liet wasn't dumb enough to leave a vehicle containing guns open to anyone and everyone. She lifted, but the door didn't open. She walked to the back passenger door. It popped open. I let out the breath I held. I didn't know if it was a good thing or a bad thing that she got into the vehicle so easily, but it did make it faster. The pair disappeared into the interior.

Time slowed down, and everything moved in slow motion. Sweat dripped down my forehead and back, my vision blurred. I wiped the moisture on the inside of my shirt and blinked furiously. How long did it take to hotwire a car? A Jeep drove by, slowly. It turned into the parking lot.

Oh, no! I thought. The jig was up. We were gonna have to shoot someone. It stopped behind the Hummer. My chest felt tight, the sweat dripped more intensely. Quinn raised his rifle over the top of the wall and lined up his sights.

A woman jumped out, dressed in jeans and a white T-shirt. She blew a kiss to the solider behind the wheel before turning and heading into the school. Neither one of them gave the Hummer a second glance. The Jeep drove off.

I sighed deeply, black dots danced in front of my eyes. I looked at Quinn.

"That was close," he commented. "They'd better hurry up."

As if they'd heard him, the Hummer roared to life and backed out of the space. It traveled across the road to the coffee shop. Tanya and Bill emerged from the building, guns in hand. Pam jumped out, and they formed a line. Gun after gun was loaded into the vehicle. Minutes passed. More sweat dripped into my eyes. Eventually, they finished and climbed into the Hummer. They slowed in front of the store, and a hand waved at us before they disappeared down the street. Quinn and I looked at each other.

"Well, that part is done." Relief flooded through me. "Now we wait for the signal."

"Where are we going to wait? If I stay on this roof any longer, I'm going to melt."

I bit my lower lip and glanced around. Then, it hit me. "We can stay in Tanya's apartment. No one will think to look for us there."

"Unless they go looking for Tanya."

"Why would they look for Tanya? They have no idea what she's doing. They think she's on their side."

"Is she?"

The question caught me off guard. I wanted to believe she was helping us, but what if she didn't? What if she double crossed us again? I wanted to put Quinn's fear at ease, along with mine, but I couldn't. I honestly didn't know.

"If she tries anything, you know Bill will take care of it. Or Pam or Kyle. She won't get away with anything."

"Let's just hope she's not stupid."

"I agree."

We walked across the rooftop to the ladder and proceeded down. There was about a twenty degree difference from the roof to the ground, and I was never more thankful to be out of the sweltering heat. Cautiously, we headed toward the coffee shop and tried the door. Tanya locked it.

"Let's head back to the alley," I suggested. "Even if Tanya locked the back window, we can break it open."

Quinn nodded his agreement, and we walked around the building.

Not only was the window still unlocked, it was still open. No one thought to close it after I climbed inside. But you'd better believe Quinn and I did afterwards. We also closed all the shades and propped chairs under the doors. We weren't taking any chances. We stood in the kitchen, staring at each other, Quinn's rifle propped on his shoulder, my hand on my hip.

"Now what?" I asked.

"We wait. You heard Tom, we can't do anything until we get the signal. We should make the most of our downtime."

I scowled. "I feel weird doing that. I feel like we should be doing so much more. I hate sitting around and waiting. It's so pointless."

Quinn shrugged. "Maybe, but we have to. Patience is a virtue, you know."

I sighed. "I guess. Well, first things first then. I'm going to take a shower. I feel like a dirty dish cloth."

Quinn smiled. "Enjoy. I'll go after you."

I showered as fast as I could. I wanted to spend as much time as possible with Quinn. I went back into the living room, my hair dripping wet, and noticed Quinn turned on the TV. He sat on the floor with the sound off, closed captions scrolled across the screen. He watched Looney Tunes. He looked at me as I walked into the room, his eyes wide, a boyish smile on his face.

"Do you know how long it's been since I've watched cartoons?"

I couldn't help but smile. "At least two years."

"At least." He patted the floor next to him. "Watch with me."

I sat down, and he wrapped his arm around my shoulder. I snuggled into him, putting my arm around his waist, and sighed. Daffy and Bugs were on the screen, talking to one another. Daffy's beak opened and closed, and the words scrolled across the screen.

"And I told you we weren't going to be nice to the neighbors," it read.

Quinn chuckled.

"I remember when I used to do this after school." I commented. "I'd jump off the school bus, run to the house, drop everything in front of the door, and plop down on the couch. I sat there until Mom called me for dinner."

"It'll be like that again, Krista."

"It'll never be like it was."

Quinn moved so he faced me. I sat up but refused to look into his eyes.

"It's going to be different, for sure." He put his hands on my knees. "But we have a chance to start over. To learn from the past and make things better."

I snorted and looked at his face. "Utopias never work. Didn't you learn that in school?"

He cocked his head to the right and regarded me. "I don't expect the world to be perfect. But I do expect things to change."

"Of course they are going to change! They've already changed. Why do we have to be the ones to make it change again?"

Quinn leaned forward and placed his hand on my cheek. "Krista, what's wrong?"

My eyes stung with tears, my chin dimpled. I took a deep breath. "I don't want to risk losing you again. If I had my way, you and I would head back to your ranch and disappear. I'd tell you to forget about all these people."

His hand slid into his lap. "What?"

I wiped my eyes and sniffed. "After my parents died, I became extremely angry. I wondered why they abandoned their only daughter. Sometimes, I wished they were damned to wander the earth as zombies. In reality, I missed them horribly. I missed them so much, it hurt. It felt like I had a deep black hole in my chest. The only way to make the hole go away was to fill it with anger." A tear dripped onto my cheek. "I figured if I went to North Platte, having to watch my back and fight for my life would help me forget about Mom and Dad. But when Liet starting acting crazy, it only made me miss them more." My voice cracked and I took a couple of ragged breaths.

Quinn sat silently, gently rubbing my knees.

Death To The Undead

"After meeting you, I didn't feel so lonely or angry. You showed me the world still had beauty, that there were things worth fighting for. The hole shrunk. Then, when I thought Liet killed you, that world ended. The hole returned, and I had to fill it with anger again. But-" I choked on the word.

I contemplated not telling him the next part. I wondered if I should bury it deep down. But then I looked into his eyes. They were moist with tears, and sadness shrouded his face. I wiped my face again and averted my gaze toward the TV. I stared at it but didn't see what was on it.

"But I didn't miss you as much as I missed them." I dropped my gaze to my lap. "I wanted to, but I couldn't. There was a numbness, and my brain told me I didn't know you well enough..." My voice drifted to a whisper.

I couldn't go on. My throat was tight, it was hard to breath. Tears dripped on my pants. He hated me, I knew it. He thought I didn't care that he was killed, that I went on with my life like nothing happened. He was going to leave. I couldn't blame him. He needed to know he would be missed, and I couldn't tell him what he wanted to hear. I didn't want him to go, but what could I do to stop him? I cared about him, I truly did, but not more than my parents. Surely, he understood that.

"So, when you found out I was alive," Quinn said softly, "you didn't want to lose me again. You didn't want to deal with the pain."

I nodded but didn't look at him.

"When my dad went missing, I lost the only family I had left. Like you, I felt hollow, lonely. I desperately wanted to look for him. I had to fight my heart and conscience to stay at the ranch like he instructed. I still hope one day he'll show up. Even if he's a zombie, at least I'll know what happened to him." He took a deep breath and wiped his nose on the back of his hand. "Helping others aids in filling the void. When I met you, it was the same thing you felt. You reminded me of the beauty in the world. I wasn't alone with you. When Liet took you, my world ended. I wasn't going to let you disappear without knowing what happened to you. I expected to find your body on the side of the road. Sadly, I was okay with that. At least I'd know what happened to you."

I looked into his face. His cheeks were wet. He touched my face again.

"It's what we do to survive," he whispered. "It's how we protect ourselves. I know you care about me because I care about you."

"Will the pain ever go away?"

"I don't know. But I dull it when I fight for others, when I put myself at risk for them. Whether you believe it or not, these people and this country are worth it. Even if they aren't grateful."

"It does help a little, I guess. Especially knowing I'm doing it with you."

Quinn pulled me forward and wrapped me in a hug. It felt great to be in his arms. His heart beat in his chest, right next to mine. He smelled like sweat and dirt, but I liked it. I tightened my grip around him and hoped he would never let go.

"Your parents would be proud of what you're doing," he said.

The tears came in another wave. "So would yours."

CHAPTER 20

Quinn eventually took a shower, and I made us something to eat. Do you know how long it's been since I've had macaroni and cheese? I ate an entire box by myself. It was delightful! And I downed it all with an ice cold glass of milk. It had been a long time since I was able to do that, too. We had refrigeration in North Platte, but with electricity being spotty, I never really trusted that the milk was all right. Trust me, you don't want to drink a glass of bad milk, makes it hard to want to ever drink milk again.

We settled back in front of the TV with our bowl of mac and cheese and other munchies. Tanya's cupboards were loaded with chips and pretzels and donuts, and they were fresh. The packaging wasn't from brands I remembered, so I hoped the people figured out how to manufacture new products. It would come in handy when we repopulated the U.S. With nothing else to do, we stayed there all day. It was the best way to stay out of trouble and gave us something to do. Eventually, we fell asleep.

My head was on Quinn's chest, drool flowed out of my mouth. I sucked in the spit and stretched. I noticed the puddle on his shirt. Crap! How gross was that? Quinn was going to freak when he woke up. I tried to wipe it away. Maybe he wouldn't notice. His eyes opened slowly and he extended his arms over his head.

"What time is it?"

"Um, uh." I fumbled for the remote. "I don't know." I hit a button, hoping it would display the time. I glanced back at Quinn. He wiped at the wet spot on his shirt. "Sorry." I cringed.

He chuckled. "It's fine. It'll dry."

"Looks like its six thirty."

As soon as the words were out of my mouth, the TV blinked off. It stayed off for three seconds before coming back on. Ten seconds later, it went off again. I turned to Quinn. He glanced from the TV to me, eyes wide.

"I think that was the signal."

My heart rate increased. "Really? That fast?"

He shrugged. "He told us the power would go out. Unless it's a huge coincidence, I say we need to pay Mrs. Johnson a visit."

I nodded. "Right. Okay. We can do this."

Quinn pulled the right half of his mouth into a grin. "It's going to be fine. Just remain calm, stay alert, and we'll come out of this alive." He ran his fingers through my hair before planting a kiss on my lips.

I kissed him back, wrapping my good arm around his neck. We stayed like that for several minutes. Eventually, he pulled away, but not far. The tips of our noses almost touched.

"I won't let anything happen to you," he assured me.

"I know. I won't let anything happen to you, either."

He pulled away and stood. Grabbing his handgun off the couch, he placed it in his holster. Then, he grabbed his rifle and placed it on his shoulder. I fastened my one arm sword onto my good arm and put my Zigana at the small of my back. I didn't bother with the holster. The gun wouldn't have been in it much anyway. I didn't realize how much I missed my sword until it was gone. The weight had become comfortable, secure. I felt naked without it. Both of us would have preferred more weapons, but we couldn't carry much more weight. We were going to have to make do with what we had.

"How do you want to do this?"

I took a deep breath. "Well, walking through the front door is out of the question. There's probably a service entrance. We could try that."

Quinn nodded. "We'll have to assume with the power out, her bodyguards are going to be extremely cautious. So we need to be too." He leaned forward and gave me another kiss. "Good luck."

"Pfft! We don't need luck! We're that good. We can do this with our eyes closed!"

I wished I felt as brave as I sounded. In reality, I was scared to death. My stomach cramped, my palms were moist. I hadn't been that afraid since the first time I went into the West.

He smiled and headed for the window. I sighed and followed behind him. My heart rate was incredibly rapid, my legs felt like jelly. It was one thing to go up against a zombie, you knew what to expect. They wanted to kill you and eat you. They were simple. Humans were not that simple. Their motivation varied. They also carried weapons. Zombies had numbers on their side, but they weren't going to shoot at you. There was comfort in knowing that.

We climbed down the fire escape and side-stepped to the edge of the building. Quinn looked around the corner toward the high school. It was still pretty early, though a few teachers showed up for class. They wouldn't stay long once they realized the power was out.

"How do we get in?"

I shrugged.

"You used to go to school here."

I frowned. "Yeah, but I lived in the building." I thought for a moment. "Oh, wait. If I remember correctly, the doors leading to the monorail never locked properly. Or the smokers propped it open so they could sneak out. We could try there."

"Sounds good to me."

We walked across the street. We kind of tried to stay hidden, but didn't want to look suspicious. Security still seemed heavier than normal, but they would be focusing on the power issue. Hopefully.

We tiptoed to the monorail track, getting as close to the building as possible. It wasn't going to be easy to climb, but there were service ladders. Quinn had me go first so he could catch me if I fell. It was slow going, but I finally made it to the top and stepped onto the platform. Quinn pulled himself up beside me.

"It's at the end of the hall." I pointed. "From there, we just find the stairs."

Quinn nodded, and off we went.

Surprisingly, there weren't more soldiers around the building. For someone as paranoid as Mrs. Johnson was, she didn't stock up on extra guns or human protection. Of course, they probably didn't believe we were still in town. And it was a high school, no sense freaking out the students. There were several people behind the front desk, but they were more concerned with the power than who came into the building. We snuck to the stairs and closed the door gently behind us. The stairwell was mainly concrete with metal stairs. We risked our voices echoing if we talked. I pointed upward, grabbing the gun out of my waistband. Quinn nodded.

We took our time going up, checking every door and keeping our eyes on the floors above and below us. Anyone could have burst through those doors. They wouldn't expect us to be there, but that didn't mean they wouldn't sound an alarm. We had to have surprise on our side. We were incredibly outnumbered. Plus, Liet was somewhere in the building. I didn't want to run into him. I was pretty sure if I did, I wouldn't take any prisoners. But he probably thought the same thing. Surely a struggle would ensue, and I wasn't in any shape to fight back. I had to stay calm; I had to keep anger out of it. If I didn't, I would make mistakes. Potentially deadly ones.

Death To The Undead

The air was thick and heavy in the confined space, especially since the air conditioners were off. It smelled faintly of dust and mildew. I sucked in deep breaths and wiped sweat from my forehead. How many more flights? I glanced up. Not many. Almost there. Then what? We burst through the door, guns blazing? That wasn't a good idea. Innocent people could get killed. How many soldiers would be in the suite? Would we run into the bodyguard? I shuddered at the thought. On my best day, I couldn't take that guy out. There was no way I was getting anywhere with my arm in a sling. I shook the thought out of my head. I had to try. We didn't make it this far to roll over and surrender. I had Quinn with me. He could help. Please don't let there be a lot of soldiers up there.

We reached the top of the stairs, and I hesitated at the door. My bladder felt incredibly full, my stomach tingled. Last chance. We could turn around now and run away, never looking back. I glanced at Quinn. Maybe he thought the same thing. He had his rifle pointing at the door. He nodded, indicating I should go forward. Switching my gun from my good hand to the one in the sling, I reached for the handle. Just as I was about to grab it, it cracked open.

"I'll head back any time I want to," the voice on the other side said.

Dang it! It was Liet. I pressed myself against the wall, hoping to become invisible.

"And if I find her along the way, I'm not bringing her back here. I'll take care of it in my own way."

The door opened further. Liet stepped onto the stairwell, mumbling under his breath. He hadn't seen us, we were obscured by the door. Quinn waited until the door was almost closed and Liet had descended a couple of stairs before attacking. Swinging the butt of his rifle, the end connected with the back of Liet's head. He grunted and fell forward, rolling down four or five stairs before slamming into the concrete landing.

He was dazed but not unconscious. Quinn hurried toward him. Liet's eyes grew wide, his lip curled into a snarl.

"You!" he hissed. "Why don't you teens ever die?" He moved to get into an attacking position, but Quinn was there faster, driving his boot into Liet's stomach.

He doubled over in pain, the air flowing out of him in with a sssss sound. Liet reached for Quinn's pants, but Quinn stepped back, just out of reach, and slammed the rifle butt into his head again. Liet's eyes rolled in his head, but he still didn't lose consciousness. He was hurt, though. It was obvious. He grabbed for Quinn again, but his hand flailed in the air, to the right of where Quinn actually stood. He couldn't see straight.

I wasn't sure where I should be. I wanted to be next to Quinn, the blade of my arm sword at Liet's neck, but what if someone heard him and came through the door? Who would watch our backs? I moved so I blocked the door. Someone could still get through, but I would slow them down. Quinn kicked Liet in the stomach again. As he curled into the fetal position, Quinn took off his belt in one swift motion. He rolled Liet onto his stomach with another kick. Placing his knee between Liet's shoulder blades, Quinn pulled Liet's arms behind him. Liet bucked and struggled.

"You're always in the wrong place at the wrong time," Quinn commented. He tightened his belt.

Liet flinched. "You're just lucky. If you fought me in a fair fight, you'd go down."

Quinn chuckled. "You mean like Krista did? From what I hear, that was a fair fight, and a girl kicked your butt." He dug his knee deeper into Liet's spine and brought his mouth down to his ear. "And you will pay for shooting me."

Liet attempted to chuckle, but it came out more like a grunty wheeze.

Quinn smacked him in the back of the head. He stood from Liet's back and grabbed the belt around his wrist. "Get up," he commanded.

Liet didn't have a choice. If he didn't want his shoulders pulled out of the socket, he had to get to his feet. He stared at me; his eyes burned with hatred. Blood dripped down the side of his head where Quinn hit him, and he had a hard time catching his breath. I smiled.

"This is an awfully familiar scene," I commented.

He narrowed his eyes. I'm sure he wished he could shoot lasers out of them.

"Krista, on my mark, I want you to open the door."

I nodded.

Quinn forced Liet up the stairs. Liet tried to fight, but every time he got out of hand, Quinn lifted his arms up. Plus, the rifle was at the back of his head. Liet knew better than to tempt Quinn. They made it to the top of the stairs, just a few feet from the door, and Quinn nodded. I pulled the door open, and Quinn pushed Liet through. I could barely see over their shoulders, but five soldiers stood in the hallway, along with the bodyguard. What did Pearl say his name was? Mark? Mitch? It didn't matter.

"What's going on here?" His hands were out to his sides, palms down. He was signaling the soldiers to keep their weapons lowered.

"Drop your weapons. All of you!" Quinn barked.

"Or what?" The bodyguard's tone was calm, almost amused. "You think Liet is a bargaining chip? You think we won't shoot him to take you out?"

I knew they would. Liet was expendable, just like the rest of us. In North Platte, he had power because no one else wanted it. In Florida, he was just a General who lost his army. Besides, the bodyguard killed innocent people without batting an eye. He'd gladly take out an ex-con.

Without thinking, I pushed Quinn and Liet out of the way. I raised my gun and lined up the sights. The bang echoed through the staircase. The bodyguard jerked backward but didn't go down. Shock covered his face. He stared at me, mouth agape, then slowly focused his gaze to his shoulder. Blood oozed through his shirt, his arm went limp. Color drained out of his face, and he staggered a bit.

"You might not see Liet as a bargaining tool, but what about your own life?" My voice was even, calm. It scared me a little.

The soldiers glanced nervously at the bodyguard and Liet. They could've taken us down, they could've swarmed us, but not without me taking out three of them first. Quinn could probably take out the others. Of course, I based that on my ability to take out zombies. I wasn't completely sure how I would do against an opponent who shot back. Still, could they risk it? Should they? I sensed the questions running through their minds. Muted crashes and screams came from the other room. Something was going on with Mrs. Johnson. It threw even more confusion into the mix.

"Drop 'em!" Quinn ordered again. He lifted Liet's arms up, causing a groan of pain to leave his mouth. "Now!"

They did as they were told. The bodyguard stood with mouth open. He looked back at me.

"Don't listen to them," he croaked. "Shoot them."

Another scream sounded from the next room.

My stomach fluttered. We had to get in there. Our whole takeover depended on using Mrs. Johnson as a bargaining tool. If something happened to her, we were out of luck. Who was in there? What was going on?

The bodyguard stared at the door.

"What are you gonna do?" I wondered. "She's counting on you to save her." I fired my gun again, this time into the ceiling right above his head. He flinched as bits of ceiling fell onto him. "Into the room, slowly."

The soldiers held up their hands and backed in. We followed behind them.

Mrs. Johnson was on the couch. A soldier stood behind her, a gun pressed to her temple. Crap! How could we talk our way out of this? Quinn pushed Liet onto the floor and held him down with the heel of his boot. The soldiers gathered in a corner of the room. I moved so I had Mrs. Johnson and the prisoners in my line of sight.

"I thought that was you out there," a female said.

I glanced at the soldier behind Mrs. Johnson and almost burst out laughing.

"Abby, right?"

She nodded.

Thank goodness she was on our side. I knew there was something about her the first time I met her. Of course, I didn't want to get my hopes up. I'd been disappointed before.

"Krista, watch Mrs. Johnson. I need to get something to tie these guys up."

I took her place behind the couch. She moved to the curtains and pulled out the ties. She motioned toward Quinn.

"Can you help me with this?"

He dug his heel deeper into Liet's back, a warning that if he should decide to move, he would pay for it, before walking across the room to help Abby. Mrs. Johnson looked at me. Her mascara ran down her face, her hair stuck up in all directions. She was dressed, but part of her shirt was untucked, the rest was wrinkled. She looked anything but stately.

The two finished immobilizing the soldiers, then moved to the bodyguard. He growled and swatted at them, but he was too weak. He lost a lot of blood. It pooled on the carpet below him, his face was white and dotted in sweat. Dark circles formed under his eyes. He swayed, like he would fall over any moment.

"Staunch the bleeding." Abby grabbed a pillow off the couch and ripped of the cover. She tossed it to Quinn.

He folded it and wrapped it around the man's shoulder. Using a cord, he secured the case in place. The bodyguard flinched, a small grunt of pain escaped his mouth. Quinn tightened the makeshift bandage with a cord from the blinds. When he finished, he tied the bodyguard's hands to his waist.

I would have felt sorry for the guy, should have. I knew exactly how he felt. The agony of being shot in the shoulder. But he planted zombies in the back of the truck, killed innocent people, and blamed it on us. In a way, it was justice. Actually, no. Justice would have been him being torn limb from limb by the zombie horde. It was still a possibility, but we'd have to keep him alive long enough. I doubted it was worth the risk.

When everyone was secure, Abby focused her attention back on me.

"You have the number?"

"Yeah. In my sling." I didn't want to risk taking the gun away from Mrs. Johnson. I didn't know why. It's not like she could hurt me. Still, we didn't get as far as we did by taking chances.

Abby approached and dug around my arm. She found the card and headed for the phone.

She dialed the number carefully and waited for a moment. "Abby here. Johnsons' Town occupied."

I couldn't help but smile. It was about time luck came back to me, and I was happy fate favored the righteous.

Death To The Undead

CHAPTER 21

I relaxed slightly as Abby hung up the phone. The hard part was over. All we had to do was wait. As soon as we had control over the other Families, it was only a matter of time before they lost their power.

"Do you really think you're going to get away with this?" Mrs. Johnson growled.

I chuckled. "Uh, I think we already have."

She scoffed. "I haven't given in to your demands. Neither has anyone else. There are still soldiers out there who will fight to the death. You and your friends won't get out of this alive."

"Really?" Abby snorted. "You truly believe that? How long do you think those soldiers are going to hold out without power? Or the people? You'll have a full-fledged riot on your hands by the end of the night. You'll give in to our demands." She moved across the room and secured the doors, wrapping cords around the handles and placing chairs to block them. No one was getting in or out.

"What should we do with him?" Quinn pointed at the bodyguard.

He leaned against another soldier, his head lolled backward. He was going to pass out.

"He needs a doctor." Mrs. Johnson's voice was laced with concern. "He's going to die."

"Sounds like justice to me."

Her head jerked around to look at me. Anger pinched her face.

I shrugged and turned away. Like her judgment affected me.

"We should get him some help," Abby agreed. "I'll call a doctor." She walked back toward the phone.

Quinn made his way to the bodyguard and helped him sit up. Keeping him conscious was the most important thing to do. I laid my gun hand on the back of the couch, sighing loudly. I wanted them to hear my disdain, my disregard for what they were doing, but they ignored me. I rolled my eyes. Whatever. They could do what they want.

Something slammed into my back and I went down, my face smooshed into the carpet. My shoulder crackled, then went ablaze with pain. I couldn't catch my breath. Someone grabbed my good arm and flipped me onto my back. They sat on my chest. I blinked and looked into Liet's face. It was red from neck to hairline, rage flashed through his eyes.

"We could have been a family!" he screamed before slamming his hand down onto the side of my head.

Stars danced in front of my eyes. It felt like my skull was being split open.

"I'm the only one who can take care of you!"

Whack! Another blow to the head. My vision went black. I struggled against him, trying to get a hand free, but he had me pinned with his knees. I wanted to flip out my arm sword, but it was crushed into the carpet.

"If you won't be mine, you won't be anyone's."

Rough hands laced around my neck, applying pressure. I gagged and attempted to suck in air. Where was Quinn? Abby? Why wasn't anyone helping me? I wiggled beneath him, trying with all my might to get away. My muscles were slow to respond, lack of oxygen made them sluggish. I thought of my parents. My thoughts drifted to the night we spent in the attic. I remembered my mom's arms around me. Then, I thought about how I slept between the two. The images drifted to the horseback-riding trip we took to Yellowstone. I smelled the pine trees and felt the cool breeze in my hair. In the next scene, I was in Disney World, laughing as my parents and I ran to the next ride. We all wore mouse ears, we panted in the heat. After that, the picture went black. I lost the ability to move. Air wasn't moving through my lungs. I was going to die.

Suddenly, the pressure left my neck, and oxygen flooded into my lungs. I gasped and coughed as my body attempted to take in the air. My vision was still blurry, but I could see Liet on the floor next to me, someone on top if him. It was Quinn. Finally. What took him so long? I pulled myself into a sitting position and took a moment to let my body recuperate. I needed to help Quinn. I needed to take out Liet, but I didn't have the strength. I couldn't stand.

The pair rolled across the floor, exchanging punches to any part of the body they could hit. Grunts and swears filled the air. My vision cleared further. Liet rolled Quinn onto his back, his hands wrapped around Quinn's neck. Quinn gasped. He punched Liet in the head a few times, each one weaker than the last. I tried to get to my feet. My legs shook and gave out. I crawled toward them.

I pushed the button of the arm sword, attempting to flip out the blade, but I didn't have enough strength. My thumb slipped off the button. Quinn's eyes bulged, a squeak escaped from his lips. I grabbed the back of Liet's shirt, pulling with all my might, which, trust me, wasn't much. I barely made the fabric move. He jerked his shoulder, easily flinging me off.

"This is all your fault!" He screamed into Quinn's face. "If you had just stayed away, none of this would have happened."

I went forward again, feeling a little more strength surge through my body. I grabbed his collar and twisted the fabric between my fingers. Where was Abby? I could really use some help. I pulled. Liet was taken off balance, his grip on Quinn's neck loosened. He turned his gaze on me. He lifted his left arm and tried to fling me off. Normally, he would have been successful, but I had enough of his shirt twisted around my hand, I wasn't going anywhere without him. It gave Quinn enough time to wiggle out from underneath him. Quinn punched Liet in the eye.

Liet fell backward, and I went with him. He focused his wrath back on me, climbed on top of my chest, and attempted to get his hands back around my neck. I tried to fight him off with my left hand, but it wouldn't move. I couldn't even lift it through the pain, it had gone completely limp. I worked on untwisting my fingers. If I could get my arm free, I could flip out my blade. Quinn approached from behind and grabbed Liet's arm, landing another punch onto his right ear. Liet flinched and swatted at Quinn, catching him on the side of the jaw. Quinn stumbled backward.

My fingers went numb. If Liet would just stay still for a second, I could get loose. He noticed something over me, I watched his gaze travel across the floor. He moved to get it, and my hand popped free. I took the advantage and pressed the button. That time, I had enough strength. The blade clicked out. I turned to where Liet headed. It was my gun. I grabbed his ankle. He kicked me in the side. My ribs rattled, my breath was knocked out of me. Quinn shook his head across from me, trying to clear his vision. He grabbed Liet's waist. Liet spun around, driving his knee into Quinn's chin. Quinn's head flipped back, his eyes rolled in their sockets, and he fell backward. I positioned my blade and sliced Liet's calf.

His scream echoed through the room. He spun toward me, his hands extended like he was going to wrap them around my neck again. I scooted away from him, but with only one arm, I didn't get far. He lunged, and I swung the blade through the air. Something warm and sticky hit my face. I closed my eyes and dodged to the right. A thud sounded next to me. Cautiously, I opened my eyes and looked.

Liet reached for me, his hand stained with blood. His left hand was at his neck, attempting to cover the gash that oozed dark red liquid.

"I'll kill you," he gurgled. Blood stained his teeth.

He made one more attempt to lunge for me, then fell limp. Blood pooled around him. He took one last breath, it made a sound like a straw makes when it sucks the last bit of liquid out of a glass. I held my breath for a moment, staring at him, waiting for him to leap at me.

A yell sounded across the room. I jerked my head in the direction, just in time to see the bodyguard baring down on me. His hands were still pinned to his sides, his face was still pale, but determination burned through his eyes. Again, I tried to scoot away, but couldn't move. He lifted his foot, ready to smash it down on my arm, when a hand grabbed his other leg and pulled him off balance. He fell with a thud. Quinn climbed onto his chest and smashed his fish into the side of the man's head. It bobbled for a moment before he fell unconscious. Quinn held his fist up, ready to strike again should the bodyguard move. Moments passed. Nothing.

I glanced up. Mrs. Johnson stood next to the table with the phone, a lamp in her hand, a look of horror on her face. Abby lay crumpled at her feet. The soldiers were still tied up, staring at us wide eyed. I didn't think any of them were going to be a problem. If I just saw someone in a sling kill a healthy male, I would have second thoughts about attacking too. Quinn stood and walked toward Mrs. Johnson. He jerked the lamp out of her hand and motioned toward the couch. She quickly took a seat. Abby moaned and rolled over, her hand on her head.

"You all right?" Quinn bent down to help her sit up.

"Yeah. Fine. But I've got a huge headache." She blinked a few times and looked around the room. "What did I miss?"

I tried to get to my feet, but I was still weak. My knees buckled. I reached out and caught myself on the back of the couch. Quinn rushed to my side, easing me to the floor.

"You get a hold of the doctor?" he asked Abby over his shoulder.

"No. I didn't get the chance."

"Well, you might want to try again."

"Where were you?" My voice squeaked out, my throat was on fire. "I could've used some help."

He frowned. "I know. I'm sorry. I went over to help the bodyguard sit up, and he grabbed my pant leg. He did a great job of feigning weakness. I heard you fighting with Liet. Trust me, I would have been there if I could. Took me forever to get that man away from me."

"What are we going to do with him?" I nodded toward the bodyguard on the floor. My voice came out as a harsh whisper. It hurt to talk. My head felt light and started to spin. I thought for sure I would pass out.

"You don't need to worry about him. He's not an issue."

"You sure? I could stab him. Just to make sure."

Quinn laughed. "I think there's been enough death for now. Why don't you lay down?"

I didn't fight him. My body wouldn't let me. He placed a pillow under my head and leaned on his shoulder next to me. He ran his fingers through my hair.

"How are you feeling?" I asked.

"I'm fine. Just a few bumps and bruises. My throat's a little sore."

I smiled and averted my gaze. They fell on his midsection. Red soaked through his shirt.

"Quinn!" My voice screeched. "You're bleeding!"

"Shh, shh, shh. I'm fine. Just popped some stitches."

I wanted to protest, to lift his shirt and see how bad the damage was, but I couldn't move. Tears ran down my temples and dripped into my ears. I tried to speak again, but nothing came out. Quinn settled in closer and nuzzled against my neck.

"The doctor will be here soon. We'll be just fine." He kissed me, then slowly got to his feet. He fixed his attention on Abby. "You have anyone you can call? Help you take care of these guys?"

I glanced up at Abby, who stood at my feet. Her hand was on the back of the couch for balance. She nodded.

"Get them here as fast as you can. We both need medical attention."

"They're on their way. And so is the doctor."

"Why?" I whispered. "Why are you doing this?"

Abby looked down at me, her eyebrows pushed together in confusion. "Why am I doing what?"

"Helping us."

"Why wouldn't I? I don't want to be trapped in Florida for the rest of my life. I'm originally from Colorado. I miss the mountains. The cool air. The snow." She took a seat next to me.

"But you were a border guard. How did you know what was going on down here?"

"I only became a guard a couple of weeks ago. Before that, I did patrol for the high school. Pearl and I were friends, and she told me what happened with Tanya and your other friends. It wasn't fair. It angered me. We shouldn't be trapped down here. I asked to be transferred to the border so I could wait for you. We knew you'd come back, one way or the other." She smiled at me. "You're an inspiration, Krista. None of this would have happened without you."

A loud "Hah!" sounded from the couch. It was Mrs. Johnson.

Abby stood. "You're not really in any position to criticize," she spoke between gritted teeth.

"You really think your little stunt is going to change anything? The Families have friends, you know. And most of the population is happy where they are. They're safe. You won't get them to leave the state and fight the zombie hordes."

It was Abby's turn to laugh. "You are so out of touch with reality. You spend all day up here in your tower, believing you are doing what's right for the people. You're not. People aren't happy. Some of them are content living out their existence here, but the vast majority are scared to death. Scared to say the wrong thing, scared to breathe. They don't want to look over their shoulder, they want to be free. They want to take back what's rightfully ours."

"You'll never kill them all. You can't. There are too many zombies out there."

"How do you know?" Quinn's voice was pinched with pain. "When's the last time you were actually out there? The threat can be neutralized. And you have the tools to do it. But since you won't, we'll find people who will."

The phone on the table rang, and Abby ran to answer it. She spoke quietly, so I couldn't hear what she said. She hung up and turned back to us.

"The cavalry is here. They'll be up in a few minutes. We'll take care of these guys," she gestured with her head toward the soldiers, "and we'll get you two some help."

I couldn't wait. It was getting harder and harder to keep my eyes open. My body was one massive ball of pain, and I wanted nothing more than to give into the blackness. Quinn knelt next to me and took my hand in his. A soft knock sounded at the door, and Abby went to answer it. Several guards dressed in black entered the room, M4s in their hands. My heart leapt into my throat. What if they weren't here to help? What if they were part of Mrs. Johnson's army? I took a breath. There wasn't much I could do if they were. At least I was able to take out Liet. If I was going to die, I was going to go happy.

Three of them hurried over to me and set a stretcher on the ground. One grabbed my feet, the other was at my shoulder, and the third stayed in the middle to balance me.

"One, two, three."

They lifted me up. I wanted to scream as pain washed anew through me. Instead, I bit my lower lip.

"Doing all right?" Quinn asked.

"Peachy." I reached for him. "Don't leave me."

"I promised I wouldn't let anything happen to you, and I won't."

We wound our way down the stairs. The trip seemed to take a lot less time than it did when we went up. It was hot, so hot, and it was even harder for me to stay awake. Several times I pulled my eyes open, wondering how long I was out, but it had only been seconds. When we stepped out the front doors, the sun was so bright I couldn't keep my eyes open. I drifted into blackness.

I reopened them to find myself in a bed connected to IVs. Quinn sat in a chair across from me.

"Déjà vu." My throat was dry. I coughed.

Quinn sat next to me on the bed. He wore a hospital gown and pulled an IV pole behind him.

"How you feeling?"

"Terrible. Everything hurts."

"That will go away eventually. Call the nurse. She'll bring you some drugs."

"So, does this mean we won?"

Quinn sighed. "I don't know. We'll have to wait and see." He leaned forward and kissed me on the forehead. "But there's nothing else either of us can do now. I need some rest. I'm in the bed right next to you if you need anything."

He shuffled across the room and crawled into his own bed.

My heart rate increased slightly, my palms began to sweat. How much danger were we in? What if the rebels lost? Would the soldiers come in and kill us? A thousand different scenarios of our demise ran through my mind. My body tensed, and I wanted to get up and run. Then, I relaxed. I took a deep breath and focused on Quinn. He smiled at me, his eyes getting heavy. There was nothing I could do if the soldiers came after us. We tried. We did our best. No sense in worrying about it. I settled back into the bed and readied for sleep. We were together. Not much else mattered. I reminded myself Liet was dead, and that was the biggest victory ever.

Death To The Undead

CHAPTER 22

Six months after our Overthrow Florida Campaign, the residents had their first vote. They decided the fate of The Families. They attempted to give them a regular jury trial, but they couldn't put together a fair and impartial jury. A vote was the only solution. Surprisingly, the people were pretty lenient. I would have given them the chair, but the people of Florida recognized the good things The Families had done, and they wanted to reward those actions. Mrs. Johnson and the others would spend limited jail time before being incorporated back into the populace. Even Mrs. Johnson's bodyguard got off lightly, and that irritated me. They couldn't prove he actually put the zombies in the back of the semi, so they couldn't put him on trial for it. The smile he gave me as he was escorted out of the courtroom was pompous and condescending. The only thought that ran through my head was that he better not venture too far into the West. Accidents had a tendency to happen out there.

Three months ago, they had their first interim presidential election. The campaigning was ridiculous, but it had to be done. We needed a leader. We also needed to rebuild the government. It was a slow process, and they stayed headquartered in Florida. Eventually, once the East Coast was rebuilt, they'd move back to Washington. That would probably take several years, but everyone was willing to wait. They had to. What other choice did they have?

We lost more lives in the rebellion than we anticipated, both on our side and in the soldiers' ranks. It made me sad, but it was also expected. People are willing to give their lives for what they believe in, and someone had to make the sacrifice. If we all just sat back and waited for things to happen, we'd still be under the rule of The Families. We honored those who lost their lives, and thanked them deeply for it.

I felt guilty for not letting Lydia, Chester, and the others help in the invasion of Florida after we promised them they could, but it was out of my hands. It wasn't my choice to have events transpire the way they did. If given the choice, I would have done things way different. I think they understood that. Yeah, they were disappointed, but they were reunited with their families. Lydia found her husband, and Chester got to be with his grandson. The end result was the same even if they didn't get to participate.

I had a metal plate put in for my shoulder blade. After Liet's last tackle, he knocked so many of the pins out of place, it was the only way to save my arm. Not that they would have cut it off or anything, but I wouldn't have been able to use it. Still, not all of the bones healed perfectly, and I had some lumps back there, along with a huge scar. I didn't mind, it was kind of a badge of honor. I decided to decorate it. I found a tattoo artist and had a severed zombie head inked into my skin. The scar travels down the side of his face, the lumps form bullet holes. It has a 3D effect. I show it off every chance I get. It's become my trademark.

Death To The Undead

Quinn's injury wasn't nearly as bad. They patched him back up and he was good to go. He didn't have to go through therapy or anything like I did. He barely has a scar. A quarter-sized discolored circle, that's it. Well, on the front anyway. Where the bullet exited on his back is a little different. It's larger, but he didn't have a metal plate put in his body. He thought about putting a tattoo over it to cover it up, but decided not to. He said he wanted to leave it as is. Who was I to tell him different? It was his choice, and I honored it.

As soon as we were fit to travel, we headed back to Wyoming. Our place wasn't in Florida. We did our part, and now it was time to get on with our lives. A few Floridians made the trip with us, ready to combat the zombie threat and take back what was ours. We never took them to Quinn's ranch, it was still our secret. We needed some place we could disappear to, some place far away from the pressures and responsibilities of the "real" world. It was our slice of Heaven on Earth.

***

I stood in the forest, a slight breeze tousled my hair. The smell of pine trees bombarded my nostrils, a bird chirped in the distance. Something scurried in the underbrush. I turned toward the sound and saw the fluffy tail of a squirrel. I smiled, dropping my hand from the gun at my hip. The roar of an engine cut through nature, and a Hummer wound its way over the rough road. I waved. The tires skidded to a stop, and Quinn stepped out from the driver's side. Pam opened the passenger side door.

"Any trouble?" Quinn asked.

I shook my head. "Not a peep."

"I still don't understand why you insisted on coming up here alone. Don't you know bad things happen when you venture off by yourself?" He kissed me quickly on the lips, then we turned toward the mountain face behind us. "I know you've seen enough horror movies to know that."

"I needed some time to deal with this on my own, come to terms with everything that happened. You know that."

I had a lot of mixed emotions about the cave. Fear and anger mostly, and I wanted to deal with them by myself. No one needed to see me burst into tears or punch a tree. Quinn would have supported me, for sure, but it was something I had to handle on my own. Surprisingly, when I saw the mountain, I felt nothing. No sadness, no remorse, nothing. It was refreshing.

He glanced at me briefly, his hands on his hips, then shrugged. "Like I can really tell you what to do any way."

"And don't ever forget that." I stuck my tongue out at him before smiling.

The cave opening was covered with a metal door painted to look like rock. From a distance, it could fool anybody, but up close, you could tell it was a painted door. Quinn grabbed the handle and lifted, struggling just a little to get the door open. I moved to help, he shooed me away.

"I can get this," he grunted.

I smiled. He always had to show off. Pam stood a few feet behind us, her arms folded across her chest. She knew better than to get involved. The sun filtered into the cave, barely lighting the first fifty feet. The other opening half way up the mountain illuminated the rest of the room. Gravel crunched under our feet as we stepped into the cavern. The smell of rotting flesh hit my nose like a brick wall. I gagged. Pam groaned, covering her nose with her hand. Quinn scowled, but he was tough enough to take the stench. We walked across the floor to the crates.

The zombie corpse was right where we left it, looking a little worse for the wear. Insects had taken care of the soft parts, and decomposition was taking care of the rest. Soon, he would be nothing more than a skeleton. The pool of Quinn's blood was also still on the floor, faded to a dark stain. I shook my head.

"Hard to believe this is where it all started," I commented. "If we never found this place, we would have never gone to Florida." I snorted a chuckle. "It's strange to think how things work out."

"We would have eventually gone to Florida," Quinn smirked. "But it would have been under different circumstances."

"Well, I'm just glad no one came and grabbed these weapons," Pam interjected. "They'll be incredibly helpful in arming everyone."

I nodded. "They'll definitely add to the stash. Once we raid every sporting goods store, pawn shop, and gun store in the West, we'll have more than we could ever need."

"It'll be worth it." Pam raised her eyebrows. "We have a lot of work to do."

"Then we need to quit procrastinating." Quinn walked over to a crate and grabbed the handle. He jerked on the side and slid the crate toward the door. He glanced at the two of us. "A little help would be greatly appreciated."

Pam and I walked to our own crates and grabbed the handles. All three of us pulled our burdens toward the door. We stopped at the opening.

"You really should back the Hummer up to the door," I panted. "I'm not dragging this thing over rocks and tree branches."

"A little out of shape are we?" Pam mocked.

I scowled. "It doesn't help that we're at what? Ten thousand feet? The air is a bit thin up here."

"You've just been living the cush life." Pam smiled. "You need to start running again, practice your marksmanship."

I narrowed my eyes at her. "Yeah, rehab is such a cush life. Trust me, I'd trade you in a heartbeat. You put the metal plate in your back. And I was working out, just not like I should have been."

She laughed. "You'll get back into shape in no time. The zombie hunts will see to that."

Death To The Undead

Yeah, the hunts were going to be a lot of work, but they were also going to be a lot of fun. We had a lot more human power, more weapons, and a lot more vehicles. I put in a special request in for the Jeeps with gun turrets and some helicopters. The new politicians in Florida saw to it that I got the necessary tools. I couldn't wait to get started.

We decided to make our base of operations in North Platte. The city was being rebuilt as an homage to those who fought against tyranny, and it was just a logical place. It was the stronghold the zombies didn't want to cross, and is was more or less centrally located. It was the perfect location.

After we loaded two Hummers, we climbed in and headed down the mountain. Pam took the lead. I rolled down my window and stared at the trees. Dust from the road blew in, coating me and the interior in white powder. Still, I couldn't get over the smell. It was clean, crisp, and cool. Not stifling like the air in Florida. I drew in a deep breath.

"I really do love it out here," I told Quinn.

"You and me both, hon." He glanced over at me and smiled. "It won't be long now. As soon as we get the people trained, we'll disappear to my ranch. Then, we'll kick those families out and spend some time alone." He raised and lowered his eyebrows in a suggestive manner.

I sighed. "I can't wait." I averted my gaze back out the window.

We bumped and wound our way through the mountain roads. After a few hours, we made it to asphalt and a main highway. I rolled my window up and cranked up the vents. Dust swirled around the interior. I sneezed.

We rode in silence for about twenty minutes. Quinn adjusted in his seat, leaning forward over the steering wheel.

"Yeah, baby!"

He pushed the gas pedal to the floor and zoomed around Pam's vehicle. On the horizon was a dark blob of writhing bodies. We ran through the horde at close to seventy miles an hour. Bodies slammed and bounced off the vehicle, blood coated the windshield and the side windows. The stench of death filtered through the vents. A body flipped over the hood and smacked into the windshield, his face flattened against the glass for a few seconds before his body slid off onto my side of the Hummer. His lip caught on the windshield wiper. He pawed at us, trying to get through the invisible barrier. Eventually, his skin ripped and he fell off the truck, leaving behind his top lip and part of his nose. My stomach cramped.

"Sorry. That was a bit more than I wanted to see, too."

Quinn turned on the wipers to get rid of some of the ichor. His side was clean, but mine streaked where the zombie flesh clung to the arm. I gagged.

"Just like old times, huh?" He pushed against my knee.

"Yeah. Woo hoo."

"Oh, don't act like you don't like it. I know you're having fun."

Death To The Undead

He was right. I did enjoy slamming through a horde of zombies. There was nothing more satisfying than watching undead bodies explode around you while you were safe inside. It was definitely better than confronting them face to face. Although there was something wonderful about shooting a creature or whacking it's head off. Call me sick and twisted, but it was nice to destroy the things that destroyed the world. Vengeance was a beautiful thing. Still, you never got used to the stench of rotten flesh.

We approached North Platte in early afternoon. A new fence with guard posts had been constructed. Safety was our number one priority. Mobile homes and RVs housed the workers until more permanent structures were finished. Construction equipment ran from sunrise until sunset to complete the town. Weapons and vehicles were strewn about in the open fields.

We stopped at the gate. Abby was in the tower. She frowned as Quinn rolled down his window.

"You just couldn't help yourself, could ya? Like we don't have enough going on, we have to wash your vehicle, too?"

He shrugged, looking slightly sheepish. "It's a small price to pay for me taking out a few of our enemy."

She narrowed her eyes. "Bill and Kyle are expecting you by the river."

Quinn put the Hummer in gear. "Thanks."

He pulled through and found a place to park the vehicle near the cleaning station. We climbed out, and several people approached with hoses and shovels. I smiled inwardly as I watched them get to work.

The three of us headed toward the river. Bill lounged by the bank, and Kyle had his arms wrapped around someone, showing them how to line the gun sights up. It looked cozy, and I almost felt bad for interrupting. Quinn called out to the brothers. When they turned, I noticed it was Pearl Kyle instructed. I ran to her and embraced her tightly.

"You made it! I'm so glad you're here."

She pulled away. "Thanks. But I'm not so sure I'm comfortable out here." She wrapped her arms around her chest. "We're so close to zombie country."

I waved my hand nonchalantly through the air. "You have nothing to worry about. We'll all make sure you're safe."

She glanced at the crowd. "I appreciate that." She forced a smile.

"So." Bill stood and brushed dirt off his butt. "How did it go? Did you get them?"

Quinn nodded enthusiastically. "Sure did. Five crates. You wanna go test them out?"

"Yeah," Kyle chimed in. "Can we?"

"Test what out?" Pearl wondered.

"The guns we just acquired," I told her.

"How do you plan on doing that?"

I grabbed her arm. "Oh, it's gonna be fun. C'mon."

Death To The Undead

We headed back to town, where the courthouse used to be. In its place were four helicopters.

"Quinn, you guys go get some guns, I'll find the pilots." I barely got the words out before running off.

Pearl and Pam were left standing in front of the birds. A look of horror crossed Pearl's face.

We all returned a while later with the things we needed to collect. Bill and Pam climbed into one helicopter, and Kyle, Pearl, Quinn, and I climbed into the other. Pearl was pale.

"I don't think this is such a good idea." Her voice was drown out by the engine as the blades spun to life.

"Don't worry, it's fine." I patted her head before taking my place near the open door. The barrel of my gun pointed outward.

The copters gained momentum, and we zoomed over the fence and guard towers, heading straight for zombie territory. I glanced at the horizon and thought about my parents.

"You thought I was crazy," my dad's voice said in my head, "but maybe my advice wasn't so far-fetched after all. Maybe your mother and I have some idea what we're talking about."

He usually made it a point to say that after things worked out. But he was right; they did know what was going on. Back in the day, I would have rolled my eyes and walked away. At that moment, I smiled to myself. All along, they were giving me the skills I needed to survive.

While they probably never dreamed I'd use them against zombies, the lessons for survival were all the same. And in the end, all that mattered was my parents could send me out into the world and I would be able to survive on my own. They taught me well.

Meet The Author

Biography

Pembroke Sinclair has had several stories published in various places. She writes an eclectic mix of stories ranging from western to science fiction to fantasy. Her stories have been published in various places, including Static Movement, chuckhawks.com, The Cynic Online Magazine, Sonar 4 Publications, Golden Visions Magazine, and Residential Aliens.

Her novels, ***Coming from Nowhere*** and ***Life After the Undead,*** as well as short stories, ***Weeping Bride*** (***Brides and Dark Secrets Anthology***) and ***Finding Eden***, are available at eTreasures Publishing and Amazon.com. Her story, Sohei, was named one of the Best Stories of 2008 by The Cynic Online Magazine.

If you would like to contact Pembroke, she can be reached at pembrokesinclair@hotmail.com or pembrokesinclair.blogspot.com

Thank you for purchasing this book. We hope you enjoyed it and encourage you to note a review at our website.

eTreasures Publishing

If you haven't read the first book in this series please check out:

Life After The Undead by Pembroke Sinclair
The world has come to an end. It doesn't go out with a bang, or even a whimper. It goes out in an orgy of blood and the dead rising from their graves to feast on living flesh. As democracy crumples and the world melts into anarchy, five families in the U.S. rise to protect the survivors. The undead hate a humid environment, so they are migrating westward to escape its deteriorating effects. The survivors are constructing a wall in North Platte to keep the zombie threat to the west, while tyranny rules among the humans to the east. Capable but naïve Krista is 15 when the first attacks occur, and she loses her family and barely escapes with her life. She makes her way to the wall and begins a new life. But, as the undead threat grows and dictators brainwash those she cares about, Krista must fight not only to survive but also to defend everything she holds dear—her country, her freedom, and ultimately those she loves.

Genre: Sci Fi, YA; pgs: 356; ebook price $3.99, print price $11.95.

Other titles available from this author include:

Coming From Nowhere by Pembroke Sinclair
JD does not have a past--at least not one that she can remember--and that makes living life on Mars challenging.

With nowhere to go, she is sent to the local military academy where she is trained to become a member of the elite secret police. While there, she becomes a pawn in Roger's struggle for military dominance and Chris's rebellion to overthrow the military regime.

eTreasures Publishing

She supposedly holds a secret that will change the face of the soldier, but, unfortunately, she doesn't know what that secret is. Her only desire is to find the truth of her existence, and finds herself thrust into a realm where the truth of her past and present is more horrific than she ever imagined.

Genre: Sci Fi; pgs: 252; ebook price $3.50, print price $9.95.

~~~~~

Finding Eden by Pembroke Sinclair

Drunk womanizer Duke, spends his life selfishly taking care of himself and screw the rest of the world. After one particular black-out alcoholic binge, he wakes to find the world changed—the dead are rising from their graves.

Lonely, guilt-ridden Hank is someone who minds his own business, and sympathetic but strong-willed Lana is on the receiving end of harassment by other students.

Forced together for survival, the three misfits must confront their world gone strange. God said the people of Earth would be punished for their sins, and so the end has come. Duke, Hank, and Lana must walk their own paths to salvation, but they also must depend on each other.

Will their salvation lie in Finding Eden?

Genre(s): Inspirational, Zombie; pgs: 142; ebook price $2.50.

~~~~~

eTreasures Publishing

Perhaps you would like to read some fun or sweet short stories. We offer several different romance anthologies. Pembroke has a short story in ***Brides and Dark Secrets Anthology***

Ketchikan Man by Ciara Lake

Leea, a young woman from Oklahoma, engages in a heated sexting relationship with a man from Alaska. Lucan, on a hunt for his mate, advertised for a mail order bride. Leea, aware of the risks, is still drawn to the Ketchikan man and his nightly naughty texts. She believes she's behaved shockingly via text, now she's embarrassed by the explicitness she shared with this virtual stranger. When she arrives in Alaska, she encounters an absolutely gorgeous male. Overwhelmed, she's suddenly inhibited by timidity. However, Lucan is patient and determined to reveal Leea's inner siren. His unique instincts tell him that she's his.

Lucan is a local artist, a talented man. He's part Native American with an extra component in his genes. Unknown to Leea, his honored ancestor passed a special gift to him.

Will Leea and Lucan's passion survive the wilds of Alaska?

The Weeping Bride by Pembroke Sinclair

Scorned at her own wedding, The Weeping Bride has vowed to make every bride from her hometown miserable until she finds her own happiness. When the groom at a friend's wedding disappears, Melanie and Tyler must solve the mystery of the Bride to save him. Time is not on their side. Will they find him before The Weeping Bride's revenge is satiated?

eTreasures Publishing

Seduced by Darkness by Cher Green

Geneva Chilton, warned against human contact, betrays her family in order to be close to the world she longs to join. Intrigued by an artist's work and his ability to capture life on canvas, Geneva steps too close to the boundaries and discovers love, but what price will she have to pay?

Lewis Hunt, intrigued by Geneva's beauty and determined to capture it on canvas, discovers he needs more. Lewis needs the real woman behind the beauty. His course leads him to her, but also to danger. How hard is he willing to fight for a woman of darkness, a vampire?

Genre: Paranormal Romance; pgs: 170; ebook price $2.99.

~~~~~

Do you like suspense with romance? Check out another popular novel available at eTreasures Publishing:

Desperate Measures by Cindy Cromer

The secret is out AGAIN...! This time lives are in jeopardy.

What should have been the perfect vacation soon became a nightmare. Caitlin Martel made a stop before meeting her family at Miami International Airport. A cryptic message waited for her. She dismissed the threat and assumed it was directed toward the brilliant scientist that she recently hired. Caitlin has no idea that a forgotten secret was about to explode and put her life in jeopardy.

When Caitlin and her family arrive on the Caribbean Island of St. Kitts, they find their dream home vandalized. In the kitchen, another message has been left. In blood, leaving no doubt that Caitlin personally is the target.

In a flashback Caitlin recalls the secret that her father, Jack Spencer, revealed to her sixteen years ago. He didn't tell her everything. Will Jack be able to confront the truth and reconstruct the past in time to save his daughter?

Caitlin's husband Scott, FBI Assistant Director, also believes the threats are related to Caitlin's professional life. Once Caitlin points out the significance of what was left in their home, Scott unofficially brings his top FBI agent, Tomas Medina, to St. Kitts.

When Tomas arrives, his status is quickly upgraded and the investigation becomes official. The third threat creates a direct link to multi-billionaire Lukas Bucklin.

The suspense escalates through twists, turns, and family secrets yet to be revealed. A powerful climax unveils an unlikely alliance between two deadly and dangerous enemies.

Genre: Romantic Suspense; pgs: 440; ebook price $4.99, print price $15.95.

We also offer YA fantasy titles such as:
Drinna by Jared Gullage.

Drinna, a young Kunjel girl, finds herself awake in a world her parents have only talked about, The Sea of Grass. It is a place inhabited by dangerous creatures, vicious enemies, and even poisonous grasses.

What's worse is that she was preparing for a rite of passage where she learned to control the rage of her people. Without the guidance of her people, the rage could be both a strong ally, and a lethal enemy.

She has only her knowledge of this place to help her. She must learn to use her parents' guidance, question long-held beliefs, and trust herself or she won't survive.

As if this was not bad enough, someone is watching for her, chasing her, waiting for her to make a mistake in order to capture her or worse....

Genre: YA, Fantasy; pgs: 357; ebook $4.99.

~~~~~

You might find this science fiction satire interesting: **Silicon Self** by Kirtimaya Varma

Anderson is developing software to speedily reach the leading edge of IT, not letting normal human living come between himself and his computer. His wife Nora wonders how dangerously close to the edge can he go, and whether the folly of ignorance is less dangerous than that of too advanced technologies? She tries to wean him away, determined to save her family and the world from at least one technology leader.

In the blinding rush to be ahead in technology, Anderson and his peers build up an expensive IT solution, but only to find that there is no problem needing it. To discover or invent a problem for a ready solution is known as "solving the solution." While striving to solve the solution, their ISP breaks down and they lose Internet connectivity. They struggle to find their worlds outside the Internet. Cut off from virtual reality, they cannot cope up with any reality, and are constantly in conflict with themselves, their colleagues, and their environment. Their encounters create comical situations.

Genre: Sci fi, Fantasy, pgs: 390; ebook price $4.99; print price $13.95.

~~~~~

eTreasures Publishing

Also, please check back at eTreaures Publishing for our childrens' titles!

Annie's Special Day written by Clara Bowman-Jahn, illustrated by Claudia Wolf.

In "Annie's Special Day," a little girl celebrates her birthday with an adventure every hour. It is a basic concept book about time and clocks.

Genre: Childrens, Educational; pgs: 32; ebook price $4.99, print price $9.50.

More childrens titles to be released in 2012 and 2013.

http://www.etreasurespublishing.com/

Made in the USA
San Bernardino, CA
06 December 2012